WILLOW AND JEFF

A NOVEL

FRANNY DENHAM

Willow and Jeff

Cover Design and Layout by Ryan Mulford

Cover Images by the Author

ISBN-13: 979-8-9911349-0-3 (e-book)

ISBN-13: 979-8-9911349-1-0 (paperback)

ISBN-13: 979-8-9911349-2-7 (hardback)

Eight Stars Press

CHAPTER 1

Agate Cove, Alaska, 1973

Fish. Another fish summer. Jeff sat on the weathered dock and poured half a cup of tepid black coffee into the murky water below. The mingled smells of creosote and ancient fish slime hung heavy in the air. Willow dozed in the weak afternoon sun, propped against a sack of salt. Dry fish scales stuck to her pale cheeks. Her long, straight hair, the color of an icy winter moon, straggled out from under her faded blue bandana.

His father had been dead for damn near seven years, but Jeff still thought about him all the time. The old man had never loved anyone. He would say he did when he thought it might be useful, but no one with an ounce of sense had believed him. What Tom Riversen had loved was making deals and charming people with his Nordic good looks and expensive suits.

At fourteen, listening to his parents fight about money and closet space, Jeff had vowed he would never own a suit. At twenty-five, he hadn't changed his mind.

He wanted to nudge Willow so she would open her arms and hold him, silencing his frayed mind, but he let her sleep. He thought about the sprawling, split-level house in town where he had grown up. Enough of his father's schemes had panned out to keep them from losing the place, but most were spectacular failures. Win or lose, Tom had always moved on to the next one just when people began to realize that he was as hollow as a papier-mâché puppet.

Out on the choppy water, the *Arctic Tern* bobbed, waiting to dock. Screeching gulls flew over her decks, eyeing her catch. The mountains, usually wrapped in clouds, stood out sharp and white against the sky, plunging from rocky, snow-capped summits straight and clean into the sea.

The cannery whistle howled, long and shrill. Rumbling old machinery stirred to life, impatiently rattling long columns of empty cans. Afternoon break was over. Willow leaped up and raced across the dock, pulling a pair of yellow rubber gloves from the back pocket of her jeans. Yanking a warped wooden door open, she dashed through it. Jeff heard the dull roar of rushing water before the door slammed shut. He would be with her again at supper.

Leaning back against the salt bag, he stared up at the watery blue sky. Summers, Willow lived with him in a ramshackle apartment above the cannery office. They ate with the beach gang in the bunkhouse kitchen and slept in a tarnished brass bed under a pile of patchwork quilts she had made in high school. Winters, she studied art in London, her mother's idea, not hers, while he slept in their bed alone and tried to resuscitate a dying business.

In the summer after Jeff's senior year in high school, his father had perished in a fiery plane crash along with a few of his cronies, one of his girlfriends, and a couple of his best suits. After that, his mother, Carole, sold their house and moved to Seattle, taking his twin sisters, Sherrie and Susie, with her. She tried to talk Jeff into going, but he moved in with his grandfather at the cannery instead.

Grandpa Riversen had bought the old pile of dilapidated wood and machinery with the last of an inheritance from his family in Minnesota after failing to drag a little gold out of the unforgiving Alaskan wilderness. His dream was to see Tom, his only child, set up as a prosperous cannery owner, but Tom despised the place. He wanted nothing to do with the fish, the drudgery, or the kind of people who worked there.

In the end, the cannery killed Grandpa more swiftly and surely than anything in the gold fields could have. Standing on the dock one misty afternoon, wondering how he would make payroll that week, he had dropped dead from a stroke.

Suddenly, the place was Jeff's, and at twenty-two he found himself responsible for everything, including the well-being of people who had worked there since before he was born. He had been struggling to turn things around ever since. There still wasn't enough money to replace machinery or put a new roof on the bunkhouse, but he had finally paid off the debt, and the employees knew their paychecks wouldn't bounce.

His mother wrote every week from Seattle, urging him to sell "the smelly dump." She hated having to tell her new friends, the ones who went to the opera, the symphony, and the ballet, that her son was in the fish business in Alaska. At times, Jeff was tempted to sell, usually at the height of the season when everything he owned or touched smelled of fish, when he thought about fish all day, saw tubs of fish when he closed his eyes, and dreamed about fish every night.

Only Willow made it bearable. Jeff had known her when they were kids, but she was four years younger, a friend of his sisters, who played with them in the basement rec room on dark winter afternoons. Sherrie and Susie had a dollhouse down there, a Victorian mansion that Grandpa had put together from a kit. Even now, Jeff could see Willow, a quiet little girl with long arms and legs, sitting on the floor, carefully making tiny curtains and paintings for the dollhouse.

Running in and out of the rec room with his friends, he had paid no attention back then to the strange feeling he got when he and Willow happened to look at each other, an eerie sensation that all the people around them had suddenly vanished into thin air.

Years later, she'd appeared at the cannery gate. Her parents had no money to speak of, certainly not enough to send their daughter to London. Her father, Jim Marsh, thought his wife's art school idea was ridiculous. He wanted Willow to stay at home and work, so one morning, on his way to Rod's Gun Shop, he had dropped her off at the cannery and told her to take any job she could get. Jeff, coming out of his office, saw her standing in the muddy road next to the chain link fence. He walked over and put his arms around her. They had been together ever since.

The *Tern* eased up to the dock. When the beach gang started unloading the salmon, Jeff spotted a new face, barely eighteen and trying to hide that fact behind a mass of curly, brown whiskers. "You must be Dan's cousin," he said. "Gary, right?"

"Yeah. Thanks for hiring me, Mr. Riversen."

"Just call me Jeff. Where ya from?"

"Idaho. Never seen the ocean or so many fish before."

Jeff watched the men scrambling around the boat. Gary's cousin, Dan McKenzie, was thirty-four, but his scarred hands, lined face, and broken capillaries made him look forty. "Why'd you decide to come up here?" he asked, looking back at Gary.

"Dan said I could make good money, then go to Hawaii in the winter. I already bought some flip-flops."

"You want to do this, throw fish around, for the rest of your life?"

"Nah. I'm just waiting for a job on the Line. My uncle's gonna get me in the union."

The Line. Everyone was waiting for a job on the Line, the trans-Alaska pipeline project. The golden ticket. The big money.

Jeff looked at Gary's careless, good-natured, young face. *Can't you see*, he wanted to ask, *the Line won't change the course of your life by one degree. You drifted into this, and maybe you'll drift into that, but when you're fifty you'll be cold and wet and your strong back will hurt like hell, something you can't imagine now.* Jeff had met a lot of guys like Gary.

The sound of grinding gears interrupted his thoughts as Paul Mitchell, beach gang foreman, clanked up on the old forklift. "Jeff, this broke-down piece of shit ain't gonna last much longer. Time you thought about buying a new one."

Paul, strong and sexy in a vain, disheveled, just-fell-out-of-bed sort of way, never looked over the horizon for anything. As far as he was concerned, every day was a fresh opportunity to do what he pleased and take what he wanted from life. That's what Viet Nam had done to him. He had been driving that forklift, unloading boats, bitching, and chasing women every summer since he had gotten out of the service.

He was always the first to show up in the spring, carrying a heavy duffel bag and wearing new work boots. It was no secret that he kept bottles of cheap brandy stashed away somewhere to warm his crew on cold nights. During breaks, he entertained the young women who worked on the canning line with war stories that got longer and bloodier every year. They clustered around him, drinking coffee, eating doughnuts, and shrieking in delighted horror.

Jeff never knew where Paul went or what he did between September and spring and supposed it wasn't worth knowing either. He didn't give a damn and turned a blind eye to the booze, as long as the work got done. "Paul, can you get the *Tern* unloaded before supper?" he asked. "We're getting a load from the airport at seven. It's going to be a late night, but we might get tomorrow off."

It was late in the season and everyone was exhausted. They had been canning late, cleaning until midnight, greasing the machines, and then canning again at eight for weeks. The work was taking its toll, and Jeff was worried. He had a feeling something ugly was going to happen if they didn't get a break soon.

"Yeah, sure, boss. No problem." Paul jammed the forklift into gear and rumbled away.

Jeff walked into the warehouse at the end of the main building. The smell of cardboard and cooked salmon hit him as soon he stepped inside. It was the only part of the cannery that was always warm and dry. Nearly everyone wanted to work there, but the foreman, John Riorden, was picky about who he would let on his crew. He already had his favorites, but would add a charity case now and then, someone he thought he could help.

A broad-shouldered, muscular woman, Nancy Palmer, was slowly opening one of the long pressure cookers that sat lengthwise on the floor between the canning line and the warehouse. The massive doors swung open, releasing clouds of steam. Cans of raw salmon went into the cookers on the canning side and emerged on the warehouse side fully cooked and ready to be shipped to faraway places. Jeff watched as she dragged and shoved a damp train of gondolas, rolling metal carts, out of the cooker and onto the warehouse floor. Each gondola was full to the brim with glittering, half-pound cans of salmon. She bent over and pushed them closer to where the warehouse crew would pack them into boxes.

Watching her, Jeff thought about Willow caressing his straight back and strong arms, but such things, he knew, were passing vanities in the fish business. Young men and women came through the front gate. If they stayed too long, grizzled men with crooked backs and wrinkled women with gnarled hands eventually trudged out the back door. It was a young person's game. Only the foolish and desperate stayed more than a handful of summers.

Over in a corner, three guys were furiously making up cardboard boxes and stacking them to be used later. They were surrounded by pallets of flat, new boxes reaching almost to the warehouse ceiling. When Jeff was alone in bed in the winter and everything was quiet and dark, he sometimes folded boxes in his sleep, stacking them the way his grandfather had taught him when he was a kid. Without Willow next to him, her arm draped lightly across his chest, there was no deep, secure sleep, so he tossed and turned and dreamed he was folding boxes.

John, short and wiry with fine auburn hair and a permanent look of frustration on his face, was marching up and down the warehouse floor, hollering at everyone. He was an unhappy man who rarely backed away from a fight, but no one could run the warehouse the way he did, and no one was more loved by his crew.

He was too smart for the job and knew it, but a problem with bourbon kept him coming back year after year. No other employer in town would put up with him for long, so he always came back to Jeff, who had known and trusted him all his life.

"It's gonna be another late one," Jeff said, stopping John in the middle of the big floor. "Want me to send some slimers over here to help pack boxes?"

"Nah. We can handle it." John shouted across the room, "More boxes! That ain't nowhere near enough. Stack 'em along the wall."

"How's Kenny doing?" Jeff asked, looking at the new guy on John's crew, a scrawny young man with shoulder-length black hair and a thin black mustache.

"He's weak and slow," John answered. "Everyone's pissed cuz he can't pack boxes or load pallets fast enough. I told Nancy to lay off him. She was giving him hell, then he'd panic and drop cans all over the floor."

Hearing Nancy's name made Jeff's right arm ache. She had beaten quite a few men at the Snowshoe Tavern's summer solstice arm wrestling contest while clenching a lit cigarette in her mouth. He had beaten her, but not easily.

Kenny seemed to exist on cigarettes, coffee, doughnuts, and, probably, speed. Normally, Jeff didn't hire people like that. They were nothing but trouble. But when Kenny walked into his office one windy, cold afternoon in late May, Jeff glanced out the window and saw an old van outside the gate, its cracked windshield and California plates barely visible through a thick layer of smashed bugs and highway grime. Inside, a young woman, just a girl really, was anxiously trying to calm a wailing, red-faced baby. He gave Kenny a job and was hoping he wouldn't have to fire him.

Every summer brought one or two guys like Kenny. Jeff broke down and hired them more often than he cared to admit and sent them over to the warehouse, knowing John could save them if anyone could. Most of them had slept on John's floor, camped in his yard, and showered in his bathroom at one time or another. He had a talent for getting people off drugs and talking teen mothers into finishing high school. His own wife, a young woman who had hitchhiked to Alaska with some friends, had packed up and flown home to Michigan. She left her truck at the airport and never came back. No one talked about her.

John's success rate with all the Kennys who came through the gate wasn't bad. They'd start looking healthier, come back to the cannery for two or three seasons, then get better jobs around town. Occasionally, Jeff would see one of them on a construction site or road crew, shouting, maybe, at other Kennys of their own.

And then there were the ones who didn't make it. They'd steal tools, knives, boots, and take off, only to get themselves stabbed or shot somewhere, usually in the parking lot of a seedy tavern or in the bedroom of some other man's wife.

"Is he staying at your place?" Jeff asked.

"No. I found them a place in town. His wife got a job at the laundromat. The landlady's gonna look after the kid."

"All right. Get him off whatever he's on. And make him eat something. Real food."

"Sure." John looked over at his crew. "Why the hell are they just standing there like that?"

He charged off across the warehouse floor, yelling, "Jeez, can't you figure out what to do if I'm not right in front of you every minute?"

Jeff smiled to himself and walked over to a metal ladder that ran up the wall. It led to a platform over the cookers. From up there he could look down on the canning line on one side and the warehouse on the other. Below him, the line stretched away to the far end of the building where there was a tank full of salmon fresh from the slime line, waiting to be fed into the chopping machine. The steady roar of machinery was punctuated by the staccato beat of the lidder. The women seated at the patch table in their gloves and waterproof aprons were talking as fast as they could while deftly adding bits of chopped salmon to the top layer of each can as it rolled by.

The patch table was a wet, fishy version of the popular table in the school cafeteria. The tough guys on the beach gang shoved or punched each other once in a while, but the patch table was where the real trouble started. Grandpa had taught Jeff to keep an eye on those patchers.

From his perch above the cookers, he watched the steady stream of finished cans clatter into waiting gondolas. From there, they went into the cookers, onto the warehouse floor, into boxes, and away, to corners of the world these people didn't care about. What they cared about was getting enough overtime pay during the summer to see them through the long, dark winter.

Jeff climbed down and walked slowly along the line, checking the machinery and the cans. The equipment was already old when his grandfather had bought the place, and now it broke down constantly. Everything was painted an ugly, light aqua color, with red emergency shut-off buttons scattered here and there.

Grandpa had chosen the color years ago, telling the family it was fresh and modern. It reminded Jeff of the decrepit cement pool in Seattle where his mother had forced him to take swimming lessons one summer when he was nine years old. The paint, the family, and the canning machines had deteriorated at about the same rate over the years, and there wasn't enough money to do much about it. The current goal was to keep flakes of aqua paint out of the filled cans.

People were busy along the line, doing different tasks from one end to the other. The young ones were bored and wished the line moved faster. They had plenty of time for flirting, for laughing, for looking around to see who was coming and going in every direction. There was time for them to believe that the turn of seasons would not bring them back to this peeling paint, to this cold midnight weariness. The older ones were sure the line moved faster every year. They watched the clock on the wall and wondered why their fingers couldn't keep up, why the water felt colder, why the breaks seemed to come further apart and ended too quickly. It was a way to grow up and a way to grow old.

Ears ringing, Jeff went outside and breathed in the cold, clean air blowing off the water, then turned toward the building on his left, the slime house. Just then, he heard someone shout his name. Looking across the gravel path that separated the cannery, dock, and slime house from the bunkhouse and office, he saw an old man in the open doorway of the bunkhouse kitchen, waving and yelling. "Jeff! Come over here. We got to talk."

It was Sammy Larsen, Grandpa's old buddy from a time when being a wild-ass in Alaska really meant something. Jeff always had a hard time picturing this shriveled, fussy old guy in an apron as the central character in his grandpa's rowdiest stories, but there he was.

Sammy had been the cannery cook and bunkhouse mother for as long as anyone could remember. The beach gang lived in the bunkhouse during the season, and Sammy was always wound up about something they had or hadn't done.

"What's going on, Sammy?" Jeff asked, walking over to him.

"It's that damn woman again."

"What'd she do?" He knew well enough which damn woman Sammy meant.

"I was making my shopping list this morning, and she waltzes in like she owns the place and grabs the paper out of my hand. Starts tellin' me what to buy. Hell, she don't even get to eat here. Why can't she mind her own damn business?"

The lady in question, Lavinia Stout, was known to all as Miss Vinnie. At fifty-eight, she was the self-appointed queen patcher and terror of the cannery. Every spring, Miss Vinnie and her deadbeat husband, Sylvester, drove a rusty pickup truck with a camper on the back up the highway to Alaska. They always found a house trailer to rent for the season, though some of the parks wouldn't have them because they fought so much.

Miss Vinnie worked every minute of overtime she could get, while Sylvester spent his days warming a barstool at the Snowshoe. He knocked her around from time to time and spent half her pay on beer, but at the cannery she rarely said a word against him, saving her sharp tongue for everyone else. Except Jeff. She knew how to keep her mouth shut around him and worked harder than the other patchers, so he let her stay, ignoring a nagging voice in the back of his head that told him he shouldn't.

Once in a while, when Lavinia was working late, Sylvester would drink more than his usual amount, make his way down to the cannery, and stagger out to the dock, looking for a fight with anyone he could find on the beach gang, his wife having convinced him that they were all making passes at her. It always ended the same way for Sy, with a bloody nose and a good dousing with a bucket of filthy water. Jeff warned him off the place, but he always came back.

Sy and Miss Vinnie lived in a fantasy world where he was her knight in shining armor and she was his damsel in distress, at least when he wasn't giving her a black eye and she wasn't calling him a useless, old drunk.

"Like I told you before, Sammy, she thinks you're cute," Jeff laughed. "Face it. The ladies like you. Always have, from what I've heard."

"You tell that woman to stay out of my way. She's trouble and you know it. Bet you didn't know she's been sneaking back there where Paul keeps the forklift, whispering with him when no one else is around. I seen the two of 'em together, looking like they was up to no good."

"Ah, come on, Sammy. You know Paul. He never pays any attention to the old bat. He's probably trying to talk her into another one of his stupid cons." Jeff put his hands in his pockets. "Remember when he talked her into giving him a hundred bucks for that ugly, old painting he picked up at Maggie's Mercantile for five? He had her believing it was worth a fortune." He started to turn away. "Stop worrying so much. What's for supper?"

"Clam chowder and mooseburgers. And rhubarb pie."

Sammy wouldn't dare feed them salmon. Clams were all right, but not salmon. They all hated the sight and smell of it. He started to go back in the kitchen, then stopped and looked at Jeff. "I know trouble when I see it. Got a nose for it."

"Yeah, I know. I've been hearing about your nose all my life. Don't let the beach gang eat all the pie before I get there."

He walked over to the slime house. It was always damp and cold in there, no matter what the weather was like outside. The slimers, a silent bunch of loners, were cleaning salmon at long, deep sinks. Ragged bits of raw fish clung to their aprons and rubber boots. Most people who found themselves stuck on the slime line would do anything to get moved to the other building, even intentionally cutting themselves with their razor-sharp knives, but some liked being there.

Willow was a slimer. She didn't have to be, but that's what she'd chosen on her first day, and that's where she wanted to stay. She liked not having to talk while she worked and was used to cleaning fish for her father.

When Jeff came through the door, the people who wanted out gave him a look he knew well, trying to convince him with their eyes that they had served their time and were ready to move up. The canning line would be an improvement, their eyes seemed to say, but the warehouse would be paradise.

He needed to talk to the foreman, Artie Stewart, who was tinkering with the fish conveyor. Artie, a burly, paunchy, old-fashioned family man like the kind you used to see on TV, was the only trained machinist on the payroll. That set him apart, and he kept himself apart, as if he feared the air of failure around most everyone else might be contagious. He didn't invite cannery people to his home and never accepted invitations to their places. He and his wife, Maureen, showed off their swing dance moves at the Snowshoe now and then, but that was about all the socializing they would do with people from work.

"The lidder is acting up," Jeff said, walking over to where Artie was crouched beneath the conveyor, a greasy wrench in his hand.

"Okay. I'll take a look." He stood up, wiped his hands on a dirty rag, and headed for the door, his toolbelt clinking like out-of-tune wind chimes.

That's when Jeff noticed fish guts piling up on the floor. "Mike!" he shouted. "Wake up and get a hose over here. Someone's gonna get hurt."

Mike was supposed to keep the floor clean, but was usually sound asleep in the storeroom. A zombie at work, he came alive every night at the Snowshoe. Jeff had never known anyone who had perfected the art of sleeping on the job the way Mike had. There were times when he wanted to fire him, but never did. After all, Mike was a local kid with deep roots and relatives all over Agate Cove, not an outsider.

He appeared, yawning, in the storeroom doorway, and ran for the hose, sliding the last few feet through a puddle of fish slime. Jeff went over to Willow, pulled a clean bandana from his pocket, and wiped a smear of crimson fish blood off her ear, the small right ear he loved to kiss at night when they collapsed into bed and pulled the quilts up to their chins.

CHAPTER 2

Willow's eyes followed Jeff as he walked away. A hollow sensation, something like hunger and something like loss, settled in her stomach when the door banged shut behind him. She bent over her sink and grabbed another fish by the gills.

The end of the season was coming, and she didn't want to go back to London. The attic room she rented there from her mother's friend Barbara didn't feel any more like home than her room at her parents' house. She felt out of place and in the way everywhere except at the cannery with Jeff.

Her father could never hide his disappointment that she hadn't been born a boy. Life, he regularly told Willow and her big brother Jack, was an ocean where everyone was drowning, and it took hard work not to go under. The only way to win Jim Marsh's grudging approval and avoid his harsh temper was to work. What he thought of people who didn't work wasn't printable.

He had moved his wife, Florence, an English war bride, and their son Jack to Alaska after the war, hoping to erase the memory of what he had seen when his unit liberated one of the concentration camps. After they had settled themselves in Agate Cove, he never said another word about the war.

Florence prepared and preserved the wild game and fish her husband brought through the kitchen door and the wild berries she and her daughter gathered, but never grew to love Alaska. In her world, "flag" meant the Union Jack, tea was served every afternoon, and "God save the Queen." While Jim and Jack were out hunting and fishing, either alone or with paying clients, she raised Willow, born in Alaska, with tales of Mary Poppins, Winnie-the-Pooh, and Beatrix Potter. Willow realized at an early age that, for her mother, faraway England was the magical beating heart of the universe.

The Marsh place, built out-of-pocket, room by room, over many years, sat in a clearing at the edge of town, surrounded by scrubby woods where Willow ran wild, wearing the smocked dresses Florence made for her over her brother's old jeans. She was never missed by anyone unless there was work to be done.

When the supper whistle sounded at five o'clock, she heaved a salmon onto the conveyer, cleaned her sliming knife, and put it in the brown leather sheath on her belt. Mike dragged his hose over and rinsed the blood, scales, and slime off everyone's boots.

Willow dashed out the door and ran to the ladies' room where she washed her face and tucked her hair back under her bandana. She usually wore it in a long, neat braid down the middle of her back, but hadn't had time to braid it that morning. She was standing at the sink, peering into the foggy, cracked mirror, when Miss Vinnie emerged from one of the stalls.

"That hair of yours sure is pretty," she said. "Makes me think of that girl in the fairy tale. What was her name again? Rapunzel? Or was it Sleeping Beauty?"

"I didn't have time to braid it this morning," Willow answered. "It's been falling in my face all day."

"Y'know, nothing drives men wild like that kind of silky, long, blond hair." She winked and gave her a sly half-smile.

Willow ignored it. All she wanted was to see Jeff and get some hot food before the beach gang ate everything and the next whistle blew. "I don't know about that," she said. "There are girls here with every color of hair, and they all get plenty of attention from the guys. No one bothers me."

"Well, that's because you're shacked up with the boss, sweetie."

Willow looked down at Lavinia, who was a good six inches shorter. "My mother uses that expression too," she said. "Did they use it in the silent movies?"

"Your mother and I are just worried about your reputation, dear. Once it's gone, there's no getting it back."

Willow moved toward the door, then turned and said, "I'm afraid it's a little late for that. Anyway, my mother doesn't care what people in this town think about me or anything else. But I'm glad you do, Lavinia. It makes me feel good to know you care."

"You tell Jeff to make an honest woman of you. That's all I'm saying."

"I'll do that. Just as soon as I get some supper."

Outside the bunkhouse kitchen, the forget-me-nots she had planted were blooming in great, messy profusion. They were her favorites, the same shade of blue as Jeff's eyes. Her third-grade teacher once said the forget-me-not was chosen as Alaska's state flower because it stood for constancy and perseverance, traits Willow knew she had, even if she was lacking others.

Inside, the beach gang crowded around the kitchen counter where Sammy had laid out their supper. Some of them were already sitting at one of the battered wooden tables where they ate their meals. Jeff, Willow, John, Artie, and Sammy ate with them, though Artie often took his food to his truck so he could listen to classical music on the radio while he ate. He could only stand so much of the beach gang and their bullshit.

Jeff wasn't there yet, so Willow picked up a chipped white plate from the stack at one end of the counter and put a mooseburger and some carrot sticks on it. She ladled hot clam chowder into a mug and turned to look for a place to sit. She was annoyed to see Paul at the table where she and Jeff normally sat.

"Hey, beautiful, how's tricks?" he said, standing, bowing, and gesturing to the empty place beside him. The guys on his crew laughed.

"Hey, Paul," she said without looking at him, then sat down and began eating quietly.

A few minutes later, Jeff walked through the door and frowned when he saw Paul at their table. He filled his plate and squeezed in on the other side of Willow. By then, Sammy was cutting rhubarb pie at the counter behind them. John walked in, the last to arrive. He wouldn't eat moose, so he got a bowl of chowder and some pie and sat down across from Jeff.

"Listen up, everyone," Jeff said, looking up from his plate. "I just got a call from the airport and that load won't be coming in after all. Looks like there won't be anything until the *Fox* gets here Monday morning. Paul, when you guys are done with the *Tern*, clean the dock, then scrub the tanks and tidy up the slime house storeroom. John, have your crew sweep the warehouse and straighten out the cardboard. And I need an inventory of how much we've got left. We should be done with everything by nine. We'll take tomorrow off."

The beach gang cheered when they heard the good news. It was the first Saturday night they'd gotten off before midnight since the season began, and the only one with a whole Sunday off after it.

Paul said, "Hear that, boys? Dan, you show Gary how to work the steam hose. The rest of you finish unloading the *Tern*. They want to get going. I'll take care of the storeroom."

Beneath the table, Willow felt Paul's right hand rub slowly along the outside of her left thigh. She moved as far as she could to the right. He put his hand back in his lap and went on eating.

A minute later he looked at Jeff and said, "Why don't you come to the Snowshoe with us tonight? You haven't taken this young lady out dancing even once this summer."

Jeff looked at her. "You feel like going out, Babe?"

"I don't know. Maybe. Yeah, sure." She was torn. On the one hand, she loved dancing with Jeff. He was a good dancer and it was special to put on nice clothes and go somewhere. She had embroidered the back of his favorite jean jacket with an intricate design of mountains and waves. When he wore it, all sorts of people asked to buy it right off his back, but he would never even talk to them about selling it.

On the other hand, she didn't like the way their table would slowly fill up with drinks, sent over by strange men whose eyes drilled into her from across the room. It made no difference to them that she was with another man. She never touched any of the drinks they sent and never danced with anyone but Jeff.

Sammy took her empty plate away and set a piece of pie in front of her. Willow could tell by the scowl on his face that he had seen Paul's hand going where it shouldn't. She wondered if he might accidentally spill hot coffee down Paul's back, which he had threatened to do before. There wasn't much that Sammy didn't notice.

"You feel like going into town tonight, Sammy?" Jeff asked, finishing his pie.

"Nah, I'm too old for that. Soon as I'm done cleaning up, I'm going to bed." Sammy slept in a narrow bedroom with its own bath behind the kitchen. The beach gang slept, showered, and did their laundry in a warren of rooms on the floor above. There was an outside staircase to the second floor so they didn't have to go through the kitchen when they came and went during the night. Sammy was careful to lock both the inside and outside doors to the kitchen after supper. When he forgot, they rummaged like bears through his pantry and fridge, leaving a disgusting mess and wasting food.

"All right, men, let's get moving," Paul shouted, scraping his chair back and standing up abruptly. He gave Willow's shoulder a casual squeeze as he moved away from the table. "I can hear those honeys at the Snowshoe calling your name, Dan." They all got up noisily and left, following Paul and Dan out the door.

John finished his second piece of pie. "I don't think I'll go out tonight," he said.

Willow couldn't remember the last time she had seen John at the Snowshoe. His wife and he had gone there a lot before she took off. The place probably reminded him of good times he would rather forget.

"I'm gonna need the forklift later to do inventory," he continued. "I'll get it from Paul."

When the whistle blew, Jeff kissed her on the forehead and followed John out the door.

Sammy had already started washing the supper dishes. Without looking up from the sink, he muttered, "Stay away from that creep. He's no damn good."

Willow got up to leave. "I always do," she said. "See you later, Sammy."

Back in the slime house, she stopped at a workbench to sharpen her knife before heading to her sink. The conveyer rattled and icy water sluiced through the drains. As she passed the open door to the storeroom, she saw Paul, Dan, Gary, and Mike in a back corner, passing a bottle around. When it came to Paul, he said, "Damn, it's cold tonight. I can't stop shivering." He took four or five gulps, wiped his mouth on his sleeve, and handed the bottle to Dan.

Dan looked at him. "It ain't cold," he laughed. "You're just getting old and soft."

At eight thirty, Artie came around and told everyone to finish up. He turned the conveyor off after the last salmon had gone through, then went next door to shut down the canning line. Mike rinsed the floors and followed the other slimers out the door. Willow, the only one left, looked at the holes in her gloves and went to the storeroom to get new ones.

She opened a cardboard box and began digging through piles of gloves, hunting for her size. Suddenly, she heard the door shut with a click and looked up. Paul was there, leaning against the door and smiling at her, his eyes half closed.

Straightening up, she asked, "What are you doing here?"

"Jeff told me to clean the storeroom. You heard him." He started laughing. "And look who I found when I got here."

"You're drunk. Get away from the door."

"Ah, come on, Babe. That's what he always calls you, isn't it?" He took an unsteady step toward her. "I know you've been waiting for this."

Staggering, he lurched forward and grabbed her hair with his right hand, pulling her up against him. His breath reeked of brandy, his shirt of rotting fish. "I know what you want." He caught her around the waist with his left hand. "A little bird named Miss Vinnie told me."

Struggling to break free, she stomped on his foot, then pulled her knife from the sheath on her belt and slashed blindly at his left hand. Bellowing in pain, he let go and crashed backward into a crate of paper towels, blood pouring from the gash on his hand. She screamed as he lunged toward her and raised her knife to cut him again.

The door burst open, and Nancy and John rushed in. For a moment, they all froze and looked at each other, then Nancy jumped between Willow and Paul and punched him in the face, knocking him to his knees. John pummeled him with both fists until Paul lay rolling and crying on the floor, clutching his bleeding hand to his chest.

"Stop, stop!" he moaned. "I wasn't gonna do nothing. I was just fooling around."

"That's not what it looked like, you rotten son of a bitch," John shouted, jerking him off the floor by the collar of his shirt. "Let's go find Jeff and see what he's got to say."

"No! I'm begging you. Can't we just keep it between us?" He looked at Willow. "I'm sorry," he whispered. "Musta had too much booze with the boys. I ain't feeling too good."

He slumped down on the floor again and put his head between his knees. "I can't lose this job," he sobbed. "You don't know how much I need it."

"You shoulda thought about that before you got it in your stupid head to do what you just did," Nancy said.

Paul held out his blood-covered hand. "Look what she did to me!"

"Serves you right, asshole." Nancy put her arm around Willow's shoulders and steered her toward the door. "Come on, honey. Let's get you out of here."

"I wasn't doing nothing. Really, I wasn't," Paul wailed. "I wouldn't hurt a hair on her head."

Willow looked down at him, still clutching her knife. The blood on the blade was starting to congeal. "You're crazy. And you're stinking drunk," she said.

She looked at Nancy and John. "How come you two got here so fast when I yelled? I thought everyone was gone."

"We were returning the forklift," John replied. "Jeff's around somewhere. He might be in the warehouse. Let's go tell him what happened."

Willow wiped her knife on a paper towel and put it back in its sheath, reminding herself to clean it later. "No, not tonight. Jeff would probably kill him." She looked at John. "Can you get him back to the bunkhouse?"

"Yeah, I guess so," he said. "If that's what you want."

"Are you sure?" Nancy asked, glancing down at Paul. His arms were wrapped tightly around his bent knees and his shoulders were shaking. "Jeff oughta know what this bastard did."

"We'll tell him. Just not now." Willow pulled her hair back and straightened her bandana. She looked at Paul. "You stay away from me and do your job," she said, her voice soft and menacing. "Don't even look at me. Next time, I'll cut your hand off."

Paul raised his head and looked at her. His face was white and tear-stained, and his whole body shook uncontrollably. "You don't understand," he said, his teeth chattering. "I love you. I wasn't gonna hurt you."

CHAPTER 3

Jeff stood behind his desk, looking out the office window. At ten o'clock it was still light enough to see that his blue pickup truck and Sammy's dusty tan sedan were the only vehicles still parked outside the gate. Everyone else had cleared out as fast as they could, most of them heading straight to the Snowshoe. The ones who were too old and tired for that had gone home to sleep and hunt up clean clothes for Monday.

He shuffled through some papers, then ran up the narrow stairs to the apartment, taking the steps two at a time. Willow had painted a wreath of forget-me-nots and the words "Willow and Jeff" on the door at the top. He reached in his front pocket and pulled out his keys.

In the living room, her favorite Judy Collins record was turning on the stereo and the words to "Marieke" were drifting through the small apartment. Jeff had no idea what they meant, since they were in Flemish and French, but they sounded unfathomably sad. From the bathroom came the sound of running water and the scent of bubble bath.

He locked the door and took off his boots, then went into the kitchen. The washer and dryer were in there, along with an old fridge, a sink, and a two-burner stove. Willow's belt was thrown over the back of a kitchen chair, and her knife was resting on the drainboard. He wondered why she had left it there. After stripping off his clothes and tossing them in the washer, he took a drink from the faucet and went into the bedroom.

Its walls were the color of an overcast sky, not quite white and not quite gray. The brass bed, something his grandfather had found in a trash heap behind an abandoned cabin, had seen better days. The room's one window had aluminum foil taped over the glass to block out the light at night. Willow's quilts, carefully pieced together from scraps of fabric, covered the bed.

There was no closet, just a row of wooden pegs on the wall. Willow had one pretty dress, which she had worn once last summer and would probably only wear once this summer. She said she liked seeing it there, hanging on its peg, even if it didn't get worn much.

He walked into the bathroom, where she was soaking in the deep, mint green bathtub, her hair pinned up on top of her head with an enamel clip she had made in junior high art class. Kneeling down on the bath mat next to the tub, he said, "Hey, Babe. You still feel like dancing? We can go out if you want."

She looked at him blankly, as if she had forgotten all about the plan to go dancing. "Let's just go to bed. It's been a tough day."

"Fine with me, if that's what you want." He leaned over and brushed a patch of bubbles from her forehead. "It's just that Paul made me feel guilty at supper for never taking you out."

"Why would you listen to that creep?" she asked, leaning forward and pulling the chain on the drain plug. "He doesn't know anything about us. I mean how we really are." The water began to gurgle down the drain. "Jump in the shower, honey. You're starting to shiver."

Jeff stepped into the shower stall and turned the water on. He remembered building it with his grandfather when he was seventeen. They bought the shower floor pan and glass door at the hardware store and tried to find tile to match the tub, but that shade of mint had been out of style for years. The closest they could get was a sort of garish avocado color. Neither of them had ever set tile before, and it showed.

Willow stood up and dried herself, then put on an old pair of flannel pajamas and went into the kitchen. When Jeff came in a few minutes later, she was putting her knife back in its sheath.

"I was wondering why that was by the sink," he said, looking in the fridge.

"I forgot to clean it when we shut down. Everyone was talking and in such a rush to leave."

"Oh." He paused. "There's no more milk. I'll go get some from Sammy."

"No, don't. It's cold outside and your hair's still wet." She opened a cupboard and pulled out a box of powdered milk. "Do you want it cold or warmed up?"

"Warm."

"You know," she said, putting a saucepan on the stove, "I actually like powdered milk."

"I do too. I suppose that's because we were raised on it." He stood behind her, resting his chin on top of her head with his arms around her waist. He could feel her body relax against him. They always joked that she must have been made for him because she fit so perfectly under his chin. She said it was where she felt safe.

When Willow woke the next morning, Jeff was still asleep, his sandy hair curling softly behind his ears and his left arm lying across her stomach. She slipped out of bed, slowly pulling a quilt over his bare chest and shoulders. Hurrying across the cold linoleum floor, she pulled some clothes and her other belt, the one that didn't smell like fish, from the chest of drawers.

She dressed quickly in the bathroom. Grandpa had never bothered to put any cabinets in there, so they kept their things in old fish baskets, the kind that were used in the cannery decades ago. There were still a lot of them stashed away in the rafters over the warehouse. Pawing through one, she found her Mason Pearson hairbrush.

Her mother said the best hairbrushes were made in England and had given her money to get one in London on her twentieth birthday. After buying it, she had spent the rest of that cold October day alone, wandering along the Victoria Embankment and eating chocolates near Cleopatra's Needle. Barbara, her landlady, had given her the chocolates that morning, along with a book about Queen Mary's Dollhouse. Whenever Willow brushed her hair, she remembered that day, sitting alone on the Sphinx bench as the sharp wind swirled dead leaves around her ankles and missing Jeff so much she thought she might fall apart.

Brushing slowly, she worked out the tangles in her long hair. In sixth grade, her friends Sherrie and Susie, Jeff's twin sisters, had cut their hair short, but her mother wouldn't hear of it, saying the boyish cuts were an ugly fad that would soon pass. By the time

Willow was old enough to do as she pleased, she had lost interest in cutting her hair.

She thought about how her mother had braided it every morning before sending her off to school in a pleated skirt, a heavy wool sweater, and thick tights. In the winter, she wore bulky snow pants under her skirt and a parka that came to her knees, just like the other children who were trudging and stumbling to school through the deep snow.

Sherrie and Susie, on the other hand, wore whatever was in fashion, such as brightly colored miniskirts, under their snow pants and parkas. Carole ordered their clothes from stores in Seattle when she couldn't get down there to shop in person. In sixth grade, they got their ears pierced and were allowed to wear fishnet stockings. For Florence, that was the last straw. When she heard that the Riversen twins were sneaking off to the roller rink and making out with boys in the back row at the movie theater, she stopped letting them come over to the house. Not long after that, Jeff's father died and Carole took them away to Seattle.

By then, Willow knew, they had lost interest in all the things she still liked. They told the other kids at school they couldn't understand why so many boys buzzed around her, helping her build forts in the woods and hunt for berries, and they laughed when they saw her riding her old bike around town, looking for pretty rocks and digging up lumps of blue clay. They were even more puzzled later, when their brother fell for her. She was nothing like the girls he had dated before.

She winced when the hairbrush hit a sore spot on her scalp. Realizing it was where Paul had pulled her hair the night before, she stopped brushing and started braiding her hair loosely. She heard Jeff moving around in the bedroom.

He pushed the bathroom door open and walked in, saying, "I can't believe I slept so late. It's almost nine."

"You were exhausted. We both were." She stopped braiding long enough to kiss him.

He went to the sink and began shaving. "What should we do?" he asked. "Let's go somewhere."

"How about the mine? But we have to be back by four. Mother asked me to tea so I can meet a friend of hers from Seattle."

"All right. As long as I don't have to go."

"Don't worry. She didn't invite you." Willow's father and brother liked Jeff a lot more than her mother did. Florence couldn't let go of the hope that her daughter would marry "a nice Englishman," something she herself had failed to do, having been in such a hurry to get out of war-torn London. The long years of rationing, blackouts, and bombings had taken their toll and, at age twenty-eight, she had almost despaired of ever marrying at all. When Jim Marsh showed up with the American troops, she didn't think twice about accepting his proposal. Her girlfriends had been so envious, and she had thought herself so fortunate.

"Can we get pizza for dinner?" Willow asked, looking at Jeff.

"Whatever you want. I'm gonna see if Sammy is still making breakfast." He went back into the bedroom to finish dressing. "Come over when you're done here. I'll get him to pack us some lunch." He picked up his backpack and dug around in it, finally pulling out a pistol, which he checked carefully before putting it back. Bears were everywhere at that time of year.

"Have you seen the binoculars?"

"I think they're in the kitchen." Jeff slung the pack over one shoulder and headed for the door.

"Okay. I'll be over in a minute." As she slid her knife in its brown leather sheath onto her belt, Willow thought about what had happened in the storeroom. She hadn't decided what to say to Jeff about it, or when to say it.

She found the binoculars, pulled her jacket off its peg, and ran downstairs.

In the bunkhouse kitchen next door, Sammy was at the stove, frying bacon and eggs in two cast iron skillets.

"I was worried there wouldn't be any breakfast left," Jeff said as he came through the door. "Where is everybody?" He got a jar of Tang out of a cupboard, spooned some into a glass, added cold water, and drank it down in one long swallow. "When did those guys get back last night?"

"Dunno." Sammy flipped an egg over. "Didn't hear them come in. Haven't heard anything this morning either. Bet they're all passed out up there." He took a plate from the stack next to the stove, filled it, and handed it to Jeff. "I don't give a damn, as long as I don't have to clean up the mess when they get sick. There's biscuits and jam over there," he added, pointing at the other end of the counter.

Jeff took his plate and a mug of coffee to one of the tables and started eating. Willow came in and got some bacon and a biscuit. Fried eggs turned her stomach.

"Sammy, we won't be here for dinner," she said. "We're getting pizza. Want us to bring you some?"

Sammy turned around. "They got reindeer sausage over there?"

"Yeah. I'm pretty sure they do."

"Well then, that would be nice. I'll still have to make something for them bums upstairs. I should give 'em salmon loaf. That'd piss them off." He scowled as he broke more eggs into one of the skillets.

A slow thumping sound on the staircase, like someone dragging a dead body down it one step at a time, made them all look in that direction. Paul came limping down the stairs, his left hand wrapped in a twisted wad of gauze and his right eye swollen shut. A plum-colored bruise covered one cheek.

"Look what the cat dragged in," Sammy chortled. "One night off and you're good for nothing."

"What the hell happened to you?" Jeff asked. "Things get out of hand at the Snowshoe?"

Willow looked at her plate. She finished eating and stood up, saying, "I'll meet you at the truck. I forgot something."

Paul, his face pale and sweaty, silently mouthed the word "sorry" to her as she went out the door. He made a beeline for the coffee urn and poured himself a cup. "Yeah. Something like that."

"You should see a medic," Jeff said, breaking a biscuit in half and smearing it with a thick layer of raspberry jam. "Go on over to the clinic."

"Nah. I'm okay. It's nothing." Paul got some food and sat as far away from Jeff as he could. He ate slowly and silently, chewing as if each bite hurt and keeping his eyes on his plate.

Chapter 4

The road out of town was jammed with overloaded vehicles, as it always was on any moderately pleasant weekend day. Barbecues, coolers, folding chairs, bikes, and sports gear wobbled on roof racks and spilled out of truck beds. Smiling, slobbering dogs, their heads hanging out of open car windows, happily surveyed the passing scene. They were all on their way to a handful of lakes and campgrounds about thirty miles up the road.

The sky, for the moment, was blue, and the air was still, creating the illusion of a warm summer day. Girls had pulled their bikinis from the deep recesses of their drawers, intent on getting a whole summer's tan in one afternoon. Guys had rooted around in their closets for muscle shirts, frisbees, mirrored sunglasses, and puka shell necklaces. If the mercury got above sixty-seven degrees, which was unlikely, old folks, fanning themselves with the weekly paper, would complain about the heat. In the backs of their minds, everyone knew from bitter experience that a chilly, gray drizzle was likely to greet them on Monday morning, if not sooner.

The caravan crawled along, moving a little faster each time a few cars and trucks peeled off onto the bumpy side roads that led to their chosen destinations. Eventually, Willow and Jeff found themselves alone on the road, winding their way into the mountains. They were going to an abandoned gold mine, their favorite place to be alone. It was a desolate place, blasted by the wind and decaying into the earth, that had once been a noisy hive of human activity. Sometimes they poked around in the debris, searching for metal balls from the shattered grinding mill, but mostly they went there to forget about the cannery.

They parked in a clearing near the road and hiked up to the mine site, their boots slipping in the loose scree. Willow wandered around among the jagged pieces of rusting equipment, looking for wildflowers. Every once in a while, she used the binoculars to scan the hills for bears. As she liked to tell her classmates in London, she had a bad case of "bearanoia." Jeff stayed nearby, his pistol in a holster on his belt. Dark, ominous clouds were starting to boil, thick and gray, through a cut in the distant mountains. He wondered how long it would be before the sun disappeared and the rain came.

At noon, they ate behind a collapsed tram tower, using it as a windbreak. Sammy had packed turkey sandwiches, apples, and candy bars for them in a brown paper bag. Out of the wind, the sun felt warm, almost hot. After lunch, they stretched out on a patch of soft, mossy plants and closed their eyes. It was the first time in weeks that Jeff had shut his eyes and not thought about fish.

An hour later he woke with a start. He hadn't intended to doze off, not with bears roaming around in search of anything to eat that would fatten them up before winter. Willow was asleep on top of him, breathing softly. The sky had filled with clouds and the temperature had dropped. "We should get moving before it starts raining," he whispered, gently shaking her awake. "If we leave now, the traffic won't be too bad."

She opened her eyes slowly, then closed them again. He had never known anyone else with eyes that particular shade of blue green, like the deep water way out in the cove. He kissed her and shook her again. "C'mon, Babe. Time to go."

They stood up, brushing stray twigs from their clothes. Willow picked up the flowers she had gathered, and they walked slowly down to the truck. As he turned the key in the ignition, Jeff pointed out the front window. "Look. Up there."

Not far uphill from where they had just been, a young bear was snuffling and foraging in some low bushes. He stopped what he was doing and raised his head to look around when Jeff pressed the accelerator.

"Next time," Willow said, "I should bring a gun too. I'll get one from Dad."

"I should keep a rifle in the truck," Jeff said, backing out and turning onto the road. "It was really stupid of me to fall asleep up there."

"Stop! See that squirrel over there on the rock? I need to sketch it for my school project."

Jeff hit the brakes. He waited, smiling to himself, while she found a pencil and made a small drawing on a scrap of paper. He loved the look of intense concentration on her face when she was sketching. In those moments, he thought she looked exactly like she had when she was a kid playing in his parents' basement.

It had taken years to figure it out, but he knew now that he had actually fallen in love with her way back then, when he was fifteen and she was eleven. It didn't matter that he had dated a lot of girls his own age later on. He had already fallen in love in a way that can only happen once, when one is quite young.

The wind picked up as they drove back to town. Jeff felt it slamming into the side of the truck, trying to push them off the road. He gripped the wheel as fierce spits of rain smacked the windshield.

When they pulled up to the chain link fence outside the cannery, it began pelting down in earnest.

"Mother told me to wear my dress to tea," Willow said, climbing out of the truck, "but I'm not going to. Not in this weather. They'll have to take me as I am. I'll just leave my knife upstairs."

"You could call and say you're not coming."

"No, it'll be better if I just go and get it over with. I haven't been there in a while and she won't complain as much with this other person there. Anyway, she's probably made something good to eat. I'll bring some back for you."

"I don't know what she's got to complain about," Jeff said, unlocking the office door. "Your dad's a good guy, she's got a nice house, and her kids aren't on drugs or in jail."

"She misses England."

"Then why'd she marry an American G.I. who was moving to Alaska?"

"I don't know. She says she wanted to get away from everything that reminded her of the war, but there must have been something else. I suppose they were in love."

"Do you think they still are?" Jeff asked.

"It's hard to tell with old people, isn't it? Especially when they're your parents." She thought for a moment. "I think they are, in their own way. They get along. They're always polite and respectful to each other."

"My parents fought all the time," he said as they climbed the stairs to the apartment. "I think Mom started out loving him, but gave up when she realized he only cared about himself."

When Willow walked into her parents' house an hour later, she found her mother serving tea to a young man in his late twenties, although his horn-rimmed glasses, receding hairline, and tweed jacket made him look older. A wood fire burned brightly in the stone fireplace while rain beat against the windows. Florence, her graying hair tightly curled and sprayed into a stiff, dated style, was holding a plate of thin sandwiches and apologizing for the absence of clotted cream to go with the scones. A jam-and-cream-filled Victoria sponge cake rested on a Minton plate, and the silver tea service gleamed.

A large portrait of Florence's great-grandmother, shipped to Alaska from England at great expense, hung above the mantel. Willow always felt the stony-faced old lady was sneering at the moose antlers, snow shoes, and gun racks that filled the living room walls and wondering why her great-granddaughter had brought her to such an uncivilized place.

"Oh, here's my daughter now," Florence said in her most regal British accent, the one she used when she was trying to impress people. Willow and Jack called it "Mummy's Full English" behind her back. If anything, it had gotten stronger over the years, to the point that many people in town assumed she was speaking a foreign language.

The young man hurriedly set his plate down with a clatter and jumped up. "Alex," Florence said, "this is Willow. She's home from London for the summer, as I was just telling you. Willow, this is Alex Cooper, the new English teacher at the high school. His mother and I worked together in London during the war."

Willow had the fleeting impression that he might actually be about to bow. If he did, should she curtsy? Or hold her hand out to be kissed? "Nice to meet you," she said, feeling sorry for him. It wasn't easy to navigate successfully through one of Florence's tea parties, especially alone. People tended to drop spoons on the floor, smear jam on the lace-edged napkins, slop tea into saucers, and run for the door as quickly as possible, vowing never to return.

"Nice to meet you," he replied, coughing a bit, as if he had crumbs stuck in his throat. Without taking his eyes off her, he plopped back into his seat and picked up his plate.

"Sorry I'm late, Mummy." Willow looked at the tea table. "It's beastly outside. Oh, how nice, Victoria sponge!"

Her mother handed her a plate, fork, and monogrammed napkin. "You might have called," she said, looking disapprovingly at Willow's jeans and plaid shirt.

"Yes, I know, but that would have wasted even more time. As it was, I didn't even have time to change my clothes. Sorry. May I have some cake? I'll skip the sandwiches and scones."

Florence picked up the silver cake knife and cut a slice. Turning to Alex, she smiled. "Cake?"

He nodded. "Please."

"Alex has just arrived from Seattle, dear. We must do our best to make him feel at home here," she said, serving the cake without looking directly at her daughter. "I assured his mother that we would make every effort."

Willow stuck her fork into the soft yellow cake and broke off a piece. It was a bad sign when her mother started calling her "dear." She looked at Alex and smiled. "Mummy is so good about keeping up with old friends. You wouldn't believe how many letters she writes every week."

Florence set the knife down. "Some people," she said, taking the lid off the teapot and looking inside, "really ought to leave behind the friends of their youth in order to better themselves. I, however, was careful in my early choice of friends and have made a point of keeping up with them." She turned to Alex. "Do you intend to make Seattle your permanent home? You've lived there all your life, haven't you?"

He swallowed a small bite of cake. Willow was impressed by the way he had deftly managed to corral both the jam and the whipped cream. "Actually," he said, "I think of London as my true home, my spiritual home, if you will. I'm hoping to move there one day." He looked at Willow. "I expect you feel the same."

Willow did not. She liked many things about the city, but always felt lonely and a bit lost there. "It's lovely," she said. "So many interesting things to see and do. But I was born here, so I don't feel the way you and my brother Jack do about England."

Florence frowned, her faded blue eyes narrowing and a deep line forming between her eyebrows. "You've never given it a fair chance," she said. "I'm quite sure you'll regret that when you're older."

Alex stopped chewing and glanced from mother to daughter, a look of surprised concern in his eyes. *Clearly*, Willow thought, *he's not a son who regularly contradicts and argues with his mother. No wonder Mummy is falling over him.* Changing the subject, she said, "We went out to the mine today. I found some nice flowers and sketched a squirrel for my project."

Florence picked up a sugar cube with the silver tongs and dropped it into her tea. "Willow is putting together a final portfolio for her art school program," she said to Alex. "The school will help her find a job when she graduates in December, and she'll be able to stay in London. There is absolutely nothing in this sad backwater for someone with her talent. She's a wonderful artist."

Ignoring her mother's remarks, Willow went on. "We saw a bear, but he didn't bother us. I need to borrow a gun from Dad."

Alex set his empty plate down, his eyes wide. "Are you going to go back and shoot it?"

"No. It's just a good idea to be prepared. Since you live here now, you should get my brother to teach you how to shoot, if you don't know how already." She looked at him somewhat doubtfully. "That is, if you ever plan on getting out of town."

"You'll have to discuss that with your father," Florence said. "When will you be visiting London again," she asked Alex.

"In December. I'm thinking I might spend Christmas with my Aunt Catherine. I believe you know her."

His aunt, another of Florence's old friends, was one of the many people in England she corresponded with on a regular basis. Whenever she had a free moment, she would settle herself at a carved walnut desk that had belonged to her mother and write letters on thin, blue airmail paper to everyone she had left behind when she married. She read the letters she got back from them many times over before storing them in shoeboxes under her bed.

"Oh yes, I know her well. She and your mother and I were great friends in London during the war."

"Why did you decide to come up here?" Willow asked Alex. She couldn't imagine why a person who lived in Seattle and wanted to move to London had just signed up to teach school in Agate Cove.

He took a sip of tea and thought for a moment. "I'm an English teacher, but I'm also a writer, and I felt a change of scenery was what I needed for my writing. More adventure. More hardship."

"I see." Willow was finding it hard not to laugh. Her mother shot her a warning look. "Are you planning to write a book about life in Alaska?"

"That's the idea. Not a memoir, mind you, but a fictionalized account of my life as a teacher in the wilds of Alaska, my struggles and observations. One school year should be enough to give me all the material I'll need."

Florence spoke up. "Alex is renting a small flat over Keith's garage," she said, looking pointedly at Willow. "I told him you'd be happy to help with a bit of decorating."

"You've never seen my room in London, Mummy," she laughed. "It's as plain as can be, just like my room here at home. I'm not sure I'd be much help as a decorator." She didn't mention the rooms she shared with Jeff, the only ones she cared about and had tried to make into a home. Florence had never seen those either.

"I don't need much," Alex said. "In fact, a certain amount of discomfort might be the best thing for my writing."

"I expect you're right," she said, checking the time on the gilded mantel clock, another of her mother's family treasures. "If you want to write a book about your year in Alaska, I think you ought to rough it a bit. Perhaps you should sleep on the floor in a sleeping bag and keep the heat on a very low setting all winter."

Florence, her lips pressed tightly together in a thin line, suddenly rose from her seat in front of the teapot. Glaring at her daughter, she said, "If you'll take my place, dear, I'll go make up a parcel for Alex to take home. He said he'd like some of my lingonberry sauce and blueberry jam."

Willow moved over to her mother's seat. "Would you like more tea?"

"Please." Alex handed her his cup. "You said you'd been to a mine today. What sort of mine?"

"Oh, just an old gold mine that was abandoned decades ago. The buildings and equipment have all collapsed and are rotting away. My boyfriend and I like to go there when we have a day off, which isn't very often."

"What sort of work do you do? Your mother didn't say."

"I'm a slimer at the local salmon cannery. My boyfriend owns the place."

Willow was sure her mother, bustling around in the kitchen, was eavesdropping. She wasn't surprised when Florence called out sharply, "Come in here, dear. I need your help."

She set the teapot down and got up. "Will you excuse me?"

"Of course." Alex made a show of checking the time on his watch. "I ought to be going."

Willow could tell he didn't want to get caught in the middle of a family squabble. He looked like a frightened rabbit. "I'll be back in a minute. Don't worry. Mother boils, but she never actually blows up."

In the kitchen, Florence took Willow by the arm and pulled her to the far side of the room. "Why did you do that?" she hissed. "Did you have to tell him about being a slimer? And that you have a boyfriend? Was that really necessary?"

"He asked. What was I supposed to say?"

"I told him you did seasonal work downtown when you weren't in London. There was no need to say anything more."

"Mummy, who cares? This is a little place and he would have found out eventually. It doesn't matter."

"I was hoping you might see something of him before you went back to school. And, by the way, I already gave him your address and phone number in London. You can see each other when he's there in December."

"Why? He's a big baby who can't take care of himself and looks like a middle-aged professor."

"What's the matter with you? You only like the worst sort of people. I'll have you know the Coopers are descended from a junior branch of a very fine old Wiltshire family. Very old."

"Mummy, everyone is descended from a very old family. Otherwise, they wouldn't exist, right? So what? I don't care."

"And—" Florence paused to catch her breath "—he went to an excellent private school in Seattle as well as a prestigious private college back East. Why doesn't that mean something to you? Why can't you set your sights just a little higher for once?"

"Higher than what? Higher than Jeff? Is that what you're saying?"

"Hush! You know what your father and I think about those Riversens. Why you had to get mixed up with one of them, I'll never know. Here, take this and get back out there." She thrust a paper bag holding jars of sauce and jam into Willow's hand. "I can tell by the way he's been staring at you that he already likes you."

"Mummy, listen. I don't care."

Chapter 5

"What did you do while I was at Mummy's mad tea party?" Willow asked. It was Sunday night, and an open pizza box sat between them on the kitchen table. "She had a guy there named Alex, by the way. The new English teacher at the high school. Those kids are going to chew him up and spit him out in no time."

Jeff laughed. "He won't be the first. Remember Mr. Perry, the one from back East who only lasted four months?"

"Was he the one who couldn't stop talking about the famous people he met when he taught at a prep school in New Hampshire?"

"Yeah, but nobody gave a damn or paid any attention to him. He tried to make everyone read *Catcher in the Rye,* then went to New York for Christmas and never came back. The wrestling coach had to take over his classes."

Willow picked up a slice of pizza and took a bite. "So, what did you do after I left?

"Wasted a lot of time on the phone with my mother. She's been bugging me to call her for weeks."

"That must have been expensive. What was so important?"

"Nothing. She was just trying to talk me into selling up, as usual. She met some people who want to buy property up here and gave them my number."

"Bet she didn't tell them your property has an old fish cannery sitting on it."

He smiled. "No, probably not."

"If she needs money, why doesn't she sell that land she owns out at the lake? Your grandfather left this place to you, and he was your dad's father, not hers, so it doesn't have anything to do with her."

"She doesn't need money. She just wants me to do something else with my life, preferably in an office in downtown Seattle. And preferably in a suit."

"Ugh. You'd hate that."

Jeff finished the last piece of pizza, closed the empty box, and stood up. "Where's the cake?"

"In the fridge."

He found the thick slice of Victoria sponge and ate it over the sink.

Willow watched him from the table. "You've got jam all over your face, love."

"Want to kiss it off?"

She got up and walked over to him.

Jeff woke early on Monday. He hadn't slept much after two when the beach gang, coming back from the Snowshoe, started shouting and laughing below their bedroom window. The *Arctic Fox* would be in soon and they needed to unload it.

He washed and dressed quietly, then went over to the bunkhouse where Sammy was mixing pancake batter in the kitchen. "I heard those guys come in at two," he said, pouring himself a cup of coffee. "They sure as hell better be ready to unload the *Fox* when she gets here. Did Paul go out with them last night?"

Sammy started greasing a hot griddle with leftover bacon fat. A saucepan full of maple syrup was warming on a back burner. "Don't think so. He looked real bad at supper yesterday and said he was gonna hit the hay early."

When the pancakes were ready, Jeff filled his plate and sat down in his usual spot. Dan, Gary, and the other guys on the beach gang started clumping down the staircase from the bunkroom on the second floor, looking like they'd had a couple of very rough nights. They grabbed plates from the stack on the counter and lined up to get their breakfast. A few minutes later, Jeff looked over at Dan and asked, "Where's Paul?"

Dan stopped eating, a whole sausage speared on his fork. "Still in bed, I guess." He looked at his crew. "Anybody seen him this morning?"

They all looked at each other and shrugged. Jeff set his coffee cup down on the table. "Something's wrong. I'm going up there." They stared at him. No one who wasn't on the beach gang ever went upstairs during the season. It was an unspoken rule.

He ran up the stairs and pushed open the door to the bunkroom. The rumpled, unmade beds were surrounded by wet towels, dirty clothes, and muddy boots. Tattered girlie magazines, ancient pizza boxes, and other trash nearly covered the floor. The stench of whiskey and cigarettes hung in the air. Jeff crossed the wide room quickly and went into a smaller one at the back, the one reserved for the beach gang boss. Paul was there, curled up in his narrow bed, shivering and shaking under a pile of blankets. Jeff reached down and felt his burning forehead. "Jesus! What's the matter with you?" he asked. "Why didn't you tell anybody you were so sick?"

Paul groaned and rolled over to face the wall. "I just gotta sleep it off, man. Leave me alone."

"Like hell. You're going to the hospital." Jeff ran to the top of the stairs and shouted, "Dan! Gary! Get up here!"

The three of them struggled to get Paul down the stairs and into Jeff's truck. As the little group shuffled past the office door, Willow came out on her way to breakfast. She and Paul glanced at each other, but neither said a word.

Jeff wondered why they both looked scared. "Dan, get the *Fox* unloaded," he said. "Don't let anyone but you drive the forklift. I'll be back as soon as I can." He started the truck and backed into the road.

Willow held out her empty plate. "Just one, please. Thanks, Sammy."

She sat alone, slowly cutting up her pancake. After a while, she asked no one in particular, "What happened? Where did Jeff and Paul go?"

Gary, who had come back inside to finish his breakfast, answered, "Paul's really sick. Jeff's taking him to the hospital."

Willow stopped eating and looked at him.

"Something happened to him Saturday night," he continued, "but he won't talk about it."

Sammy turned around, spatula in hand. "I thought he got in a fight at the Snowshoe. That's what he said yesterday morning."

Gary got up to take his dirty dishes to the sink. "That ain't right. He wasn't at the Snowshoe Saturday night. Don't know where he was. When we got back, he was already in his room with the door shut."

Willow put her plate on the counter. "Thanks, Sammy. You make the best pancakes."

As she ran to the slime house, the whistle began to howl. She put on her apron and gloves, went to her sink, and pulled a fish off the conveyor. She tried to think about the painting she was going to make of the squirrel they had seen near the mine, but couldn't stop thinking about Jeff driving Paul to the hospital.

When the whistle blew at ten for morning break, she went with the other slimers to the break room and got a packet of powdered cocoa mix. She tore it open, dumped it into a cup, and added hot water. Jeff wasn't back, so she went to sit with Nancy in the warehouse. "Did you hear about Paul?" she asked. "Jeff had to take him to the hospital this morning."

"Yeah? What's wrong with him?" Nancy dunked a piece of doughnut in her coffee. "We didn't hurt him that bad. Just taught him a lesson."

"We better tell Jeff what happened."

Nancy finished her coffee and stood up. "Okay. Best if we tell our story first anyway." She brushed some sugar off her red-and-black plaid shirt. "Once Paul starts lying, the whole beach gang will be out to get us."

Jeff tried to focus on the stack of papers on his desk. He had left Paul at the hospital after he was admitted and rolled away on a gurney. They had started him on antibiotics for a bad case of fish poisoning and were going to stitch up a shallow cut on his hand. He refused to tell anyone how he had gotten injured, saying over and over that he didn't remember.

When the whistle blew for lunch, he was still at his desk, having worked his way through more than half the papers. The business was doing a lot better now than when his grandfather was in charge. *My mother should be proud of me*, he thought, looking at a new letter from her that he had put off opening.

As he pushed his chair back and got up to go to lunch, the door opened, and Willow, Nancy, and John walked in. He sat down again.

John spoke first. "Hey, Jeff. How's Paul? We heard you took him to the hospital."

"They said he'll be okay. He's got a nasty case of fish poisoning and a cut on his hand." He looked at each of them in turn. "And a bruised foot and a black eye." He paused. "Is that why you're here, to find out about Paul?"

"We need to tell you about something," Nancy said. "Something that happened Saturday night when we were shutting down."

"Okay."

To Jeff's surprise, Willow spoke next. "I did it," she said in a faint voice. "I cut Paul's hand. He grabbed my hair and was pushing me around in the storeroom. He wouldn't let go even after I yelled and stomped on his foot, so I pulled out my knife and cut him. Then Nancy and John showed up."

No one said anything, so she went on. "He was really drunk. I saw him guzzling brandy with Mike and Dan and Gary after dinner."

"We were bringing the forklift back," John said. "We'd borrowed it to take inventory."

"When we heard Willow yelling, we ran in the slime house," Nancy added. "Paul's hand was bleeding like stink when we got there. It wasn't hard to figure out what was going on. I punched him in the face, then John worked him over a bit."

"The bastard had it coming," John said.

Jeff glared at them. "Why didn't you tell me before now?"

"Because Paul started crying after Nancy and John hit him," Willow said and looked down at the desk. "He was rolling around on the floor and sobbing about not wanting to lose his job. It was sad."

"He was blaming Miss Vinnie," Nancy said. "Said she'd put him up to it by telling him Willow was sweet on him."

"Come here, Babe." Jeff gestured at Willow. She walked around the desk and sat down in his lap. He put his arms around her tightly. "All right. You two go get lunch. And don't discuss this with anyone. I need to think things over."

Nancy and John left the office, closing the door behind them. Jeff kissed Willow's head gently, saying, "It's all right. Go upstairs. I'll get some lunch and bring it over."

Over in the bunkhouse, everyone was eating tomato soup and grilled cheese sandwiches. Sammy was slicing apples and cutting brownies at the back counter when Jeff walked in.

"Sammy, I need to take lunch upstairs for Willow and me. Can you pack up something?" His voice had a hard edge to it.

Dan looked up. "What's the word on Paul? Is he gonna be okay?"

"Yeah. He's got a really bad case of fish poisoning." He looked around the room. "I don't ever want to catch any of you being so stupid. If you've got fish poisoning, get over to the clinic right away."

Gary stopped slurping his soup. "What's fish poisoning?"

Dan answered. "It's when you get fish juice in a cut and it gets infected. You gotta get medicine right away or it'll get in your blood and kill you."

"Really? Jeez. Didn't Paul know about that?"

"Sure he did. He was just being a dumbass as usual."

Sammy handed Jeff a thermos of soup and a bag with the rest of their lunch in it. "Thanks, Sammy. Dan, I'll be at my place for a while. You know what has to get done."

Upstairs, Willow sat at the kitchen table, drinking a cup of hot Russian tea, a mixture of Tang, spices, and instant tea that she loved and her mother detested.

When Jeff walked in, she looked up. She wanted to ask him to climb in bed and hold her without talking, but that would have to wait. He poured soup into two bowls and set one in front of her.

"Thanks. This looks great."

He put the rest of their lunch on the table and sat down across from her. "You should have told me."

"I'm sorry. It was scary at first, but then I ended up just feeling sorry for him." She took a bite of grilled cheese and chewed it slowly.

Jeff picked up his soup spoon. "He tried to hurt you, Babe."

"What if he dies from the fish poisoning? Does that mean I killed him?"

"What? He didn't get fish poisoning from anything you did. He already had a bunch of infected cuts on his arms that he was ignoring. He should have gotten his hand looked at after you cut it, but that's not what made him sick."

Willow felt a small wave of relief. "How'd he get those other cuts?"

"Who knows? Probably from unloading one of the boats a week or two ago." Jeff reached across the table and took her hand. "I'd love to beat the crap out of him, but I'm not going to. I'm just gonna make sure he leaves town and never comes back. You won't ever see him again."

"I can't figure out why he said it was all Miss Vinnie's fault."

"I don't know about that either, but I'm going to find out." Jeff took the bowls to the sink. "I should have gotten rid of both of them years ago. You stay up here this afternoon and listen to some music or something."

"No, I'm going back to work. I'm okay."

"All right," he said, picking up a brownie. "I'll see you later."

Chapter 6

Jeff stuck his hands in his pockets and walked over to the break room to look for Miss Vinnie. A biting wind blew off the water, making him wish he had put on his down vest. Only a few hardy souls were eating outside and the break room was packed. People who hadn't managed to snag a place on a bench leaned against the whitewashed walls, munching their sandwiches and hard-boiled eggs. The crowded room smelled of fish, rubber boots, and peanut butter. Everyone stopped talking when Jeff appeared in the doorway.

"Anyone know where Lavinia is?" he asked.

"She was here this morning," answered a young woman peeling an orange in the back corner. He recognized her as one of the new patchers.

"I saw her leave a few minutes ago. There was a car waiting outside the gate when we got off for lunch," Kenny said. Jeff was surprised to see him in there. The warehouse crew usually ate by themselves.

"Okay. Thanks." He turned around and went over to the bunkhouse. Artie was leaving when he got there. "I'm going over to Lavinia's place," Jeff said. "It looks like she took off without telling anyone. I'm going to fire her."

"Oh yeah? What's going on?" Artie asked.

"I'll tell you later. Keep an eye on things. If Willow looks like she's having a bad afternoon, make her stop and go upstairs."

Artie looked even more suspicious and puzzled when he heard that. His eyes narrowed as he stood directly in front of Jeff, blocking his path. "Is she all right? What's the matter with everyone today?"

Jeff stepped around him. "I'll tell you when I get back."

After he had driven halfway to town, he realized that he didn't know which trailer park Miss Vinnie and Sylvester were living in that summer. They had been banned from some of them because the managers didn't like the police coming around, and no one wanted to get in the middle of their domestic disputes.

As he got closer to town, he remembered Lavinia telling a story about how she and Sylvester liked to take lawn chairs and a six-pack of beer out to a clearing in the woods where they could watch X-rated movies for free at the drive-in next door. They couldn't hear the sound, so they made up their own words to go with the heaving breasts and buttocks on the outdoor screen. Jeff had no trouble finding the right place after that.

He pulled into the gravel parking lot and stopped in front of a flat-roofed, cinder block building. The place had one dirty window in front and a sign on the door that said "Office." Inside, he found the manager, a short, balding guy of about fifty, slumped in a ripped armchair behind the counter. He was studying the want ads in the weekly paper. Looking over the top of his reading glasses, he asked, "Can I help you?"

"I'm looking for Lavinia Stout. She works for me."

"Is she in trouble?" he asked eagerly. Jeff wondered if he was looking for a reason to get rid of the Stouts.

"Only with me. Nothing to do with you or the law."

Getting up from his chair, the manager pointed toward the back of the building. "Space seventeen. That way. Watch out for the neighbor's dog," he said, reaching under the counter for a handful of dog biscuits. "He doesn't usually bite, but take some of these anyway. His name's Charlie. Just tell him to shut up and throw him a few of these if he starts barking. He's on a chain, so you'll be okay if you keep your distance."

"Thanks." Jeff stuffed the biscuits in his shirt pocket and went around back to look for space seventeen. Most of the trailers were the same color and size, their foundations encircled by thick clumps of dandelions and clover. Lawn chairs with frayed webbing, empty propane tanks, rusty barbecues, trikes, and other outdoor items in various states of decay and disrepair littered the ground around them.

He kept walking until he found the right area. Pulling a few dog biscuits from his pocket, he scanned the neighbor's yard for Charlie. There was a long, heavy chain lying in the uncut grass, but no sign of the dog. He noticed that the far end of the chain was firmly bolted to the roof of an empty doghouse. *Poor mutt,* he thought, *no wonder he goes crazy when people wander by.*

He was startled to see that someone, presumably Miss Vinnie, had tried to make their trailer more attractive than the others. An old wheelbarrow near the door had been painted bright blue and turned into a planter with pink geraniums cascading over its sides. Baskets of begonias hung on chains from hooks under the eaves. A homemade, varnished wood plaque near the door proclaimed this to be the abode of "Sy & Vinnie."

Jeff knocked loudly and heard feet scampering across the floor, but no one came to the door. Looking to the left, he saw a sheer window curtain twitch slightly behind the glass. "Lavinia, I know you're in there!" he shouted. "Open the door!"

As he raised his fist to pound on the door again, it opened and Lavinia stuck her head out. "Shush! You'll wake Sylvester. What are you doing here?"

"What are *you* doing here?" he said angrily. "You're supposed to be at work. Why'd you take off without telling anyone?"

"I'm not feeling good. You better go." She started to close the door in his face.

"I'm not going anywhere, Lavinia. Either you let me in and tell me why you stirred up all this trouble with Paul or I'm gonna make enough noise to wake that louse and all his drinking buddies for miles around."

After pondering this for a moment, she slowly opened the door. "All right. Come in. But promise you'll be quiet."

Inside, Jeff heard loud snoring coming from somewhere down the hall. Lavinia rushed past him, saying, "Have a seat in the kitchen while I shut the bedroom door."

Returning a minute later, she asked, "Want a beer?"

"Lavinia, it's lunchtime and it's a work day. No, I don't want a beer. Would you please sit down?"

After fussing a bit at the sink, she sat down. The inside of the trailer, like the outside, surprised him. In the living room there were starched lace doilies under the table lamps and crocheted afghans on the sofa. Ruffled curtains covered the windows, and vases of artificial flowers were scattered around the room. A purple shag rug covered most of the living room floor and a cluster of glass grapes sat on the kitchen table. A half dozen delicate china teacups hung on hooks under one of the kitchen cabinets.

As Lavinia nervously reached across the table to adjust the grapes, Jeff saw the greenish-yellow edge of a large bruise peeking out from under the cuff of her right sleeve. He was pretty sure she hadn't gotten it sitting at the patch table in the cannery. "Tell me what's going on," he said, "or I'm going to have to let you go."

She looked at her manicured red nails for a moment, then pushed a loose hair pin back into her gray hair. "I heard about Paul going to the hospital. Is it true about him and Willow?"

"What did you hear?"

"That he tried to force himself on her, and she cut his hand with her knife."

"Who told you that?"

"I don't know. Seems like everyone was talking about it this morning."

"What I heard was that you put Paul up to it."

She looked up indignantly. "Who said that?"

"Never mind. Is it true?"

She stood up and went to the fridge. "You sure you don't want a beer? I think I'll just get one for myself if you don't mind."

"Listen to me, damn it! I'm asking why you did it. Why'd you tell Paul a pack of lies?"

Startled, she turned and looked at him. "Hush! Keep your voice down. I didn't tell him to grab her or push himself on her. What kind of woman do you think I am?"

"I don't know, Lavinia. I really don't. Just tell me what you did. I've got to get back to work."

She poured a beer into a tall glass and brought it to the table. "I told him I thought she liked him, and he should try making a pass at her." She took a long drink, set her glass down, and looked at him defiantly.

"You know that's a lie."

"Is it?"

"You know it is. Why'd you do it?"

Lavinia stared silently into her lap. Slowly, a few tears began to run down her cheeks, spotting her lavender stretch pants and pink polyester shirt. "It's because of Darlene. Because you wouldn't fire her," she sniffed, reaching into one of her pockets for a tissue.

"What are you talking about? You mean Darlene Simmons in the can shop?" Jeff was picturing a small woman of about Lavinia's age, but thinner and flashier, who had been running one of the can reformers for a summer or two. She was notorious for flirting with any male over the age of fifteen, saying it made the time pass more quickly. Feeding flat cans into the deafening reformer, hour after hour, was an awful job. No one ever paid any attention to Darlene.

"I told you she was causing trouble and asked you to fire her. Don't you remember?" Lavinia blew her nose into the tissue and got up to throw it away. "Now see what's happened?"

Jeff leaned back in his chair and studied a framed black velvet painting of a matador on the kitchen wall. "There was no reason to fire her. I can't get rid of people just because you don't like them. What does my not firing Darlene have to do with anything? I don't get it."

"Well, she and Sylvester, they've been, you know, sneaking off together." Tearing a paper towel off the roll near the sink, she dabbed her eyes and said in a choked voice, "I thought if I could get you to fire her, she would leave town and that would put a stop to it."

"And when I wouldn't do it, you decided to get even with me. Is that it?"

She began noisily washing her beer glass in the sink. "I never thought anyone would get hurt. I just wanted you to feel a little jealous, a little miserable. You two always look like you're so damn in love. How do you think that makes the rest of us feel? You never fight and you're always out there on the dock cuddling and kissing. It makes me sick."

Jeff pushed his chair back and stood up. He didn't know what to say. It had never crossed his mind that people like Miss Vinnie were watching him so closely and thinking things like that. He felt embarrassed and violated at the same time, suddenly aware that dozens of prying eyes had been following his every move.

"So, am I fired?" Lavinia sniffled. "We can't get by on Sylvester's pension alone. You know he's got a bad back and bad knees, and I've got to work. I swear I won't cause any more trouble."

"You got two people, including the woman I love more than anything in the world, injured because you thought that old bum of yours was seeing Darlene behind your back?!" Jeff yelled. "Is that it? You should have dumped him years ago!"

As soon as the words were out of his mouth, he regretted it. Why did the romantic troubles of old people seem so ridiculous? Was it because they were no longer even vaguely attractive to anyone but each other? One day, he and Willow would be old, and their love story would make the young people around them cringe. No one would want to think about it any more than he wanted to think about Lavinia and Darlene being in love with Sylvester.

She burst into tears, sobbing into a cotton dish towel, her shoulders shaking. "Please, Jeff. I never thought Paul would do anything so terrible."

A door opened down the hall, and Jeff heard footsteps coming toward the kitchen. Sylvester, dressed in tight white underpants, black socks, and a gray t-shirt, padded into the room. His belly hung over his waistband and he badly needed a shave. Glaring at Jeff with bloodshot eyes, he asked, "What the hell's going on? What are you doing here?"

Lavinia dried her eyes quickly and smiled at him. "I wasn't feeling too good this morning, honey, so I got a ride home. Jeff just stopped by to check on me. Isn't that nice?"

Sylvester grunted. "You want a beer?" he asked, making his way to the fridge.

"No thanks. I'm leaving." As he went out the door, Jeff looked back at Miss Vinnie. "Come back to work tomorrow if you're feeling better."

Outside, he looked at the geraniums in the blue wheelbarrow and tried to clear his head. There was still no sign of Charlie, so he went over to the doghouse and tossed the dog biscuits the manager had given him into a metal food bowl.

CHAPTER 7

Willow bent over her sink, shifting her weight from one cold foot to the other, trying to stay awake. Jeff had tossed and turned all night, twisting the covers and getting up again and again to wander aimlessly around the apartment. She knew he was thinking about Paul.

Feeling a light tap on her shoulder, she stopped working and looked up. Artie was standing next to her. "There's a guy here says he wants to talk to you. Strange-looking fellow. Outsider."

"What? Now?"

"Yeah. Go on."

She got cleaned up and went outside. Alex was by the gate, standing next to a brown station wagon that she knew belonged to Keith, his landlord. He smiled and waved. Puzzled, she walked over to him. "Alex? What are you doing here?"

"Keith said I could borrow his car for a couple of hours. I was hoping you'd show me around town. Your mother suggested it when I took her flowers this morning to thank her for tea on Sunday."

"That was nice of you, but I'm sorry, I can't leave now. We're really busy."

"She said you could leave whenever you wanted to because of, you know, your connection to the owner."

"She shouldn't have said that. I'm sorry."

Just then the ten o'clock whistle blew for morning break.

Alex jumped. "What was that?"

"Nothing. Just the break whistle."

"Are you sure you can't get away? I'm meeting my new work colleagues this afternoon and I'd like them to think I know something about this place, that I'm not as much of an outsider as I seem. That's what you call people like me, isn't it? Outsiders. I've learned that much since I saw you on Sunday."

Noting the bitter tone in his voice, Willow wondered if Alex might be the kind of guy who always felt like an outsider. "That's true," she said, "but don't feel bad about it. There are people who've lived here for years and everyone still calls them outsiders."

"Is that supposed to make me feel better?"

She smiled. "Sorry. Okay, I'll see what I can do. Wait here." She knew she could leave without telling anyone, but if Miss Vinnie found out, she'd complain, and Jeff didn't need that, so she went looking for him, first in the office and then in the bunkhouse kitchen where Sammy was filling a stew pot with beef and vegetables. "Hi, Sammy. What smells so good?"

"Oatmeal raisin cookies in the oven."

"Have you seen Jeff?"

"He's out on the dock, talkin' to the captain of the *Kerry Ann*."

"Will you tell him I had to go into town? I won't be away long."

"This got somethin' to do with that outsider by the gate?"

"Yeah. My mother is meddling again."

A few minutes later, having dashed up to the apartment to change into clean clothes, she joined Alex at the gate.

"Perhaps you should drive," he said, handing her the keys. "You know where to go."

"All right." She opened the driver's side door. "What do you want to see? It's not a big place."

"Whatever you think I should see." He got into the passenger seat and rolled the window down. "How about your grade school or some places you went to have fun when you were a kid? I'm seeing the high school this afternoon."

"Okay, but you won't be impressed. This isn't Seattle." She backed out and headed for town. "We don't have tall buildings or mansions, but you probably figured that out already. The fanciest place in town is the movie theater."

"Then let's go there. Did you go to the movies a lot when you were growing up?"

"No. It was too expensive, and my father thinks movies are a waste of time. But I was there on Good Friday in '64, not long before the big earthquake hit. My mother wouldn't give me money for popcorn, which she thinks is garbage, so my friends and I made it at one of their houses and snuck it in under our coats. I'd just gotten home when the house started shaking. It was strange and terrifying at the same time. After it was over, there wasn't any clean water coming out of the faucets, so we had to carry buckets of snow inside and add drops of bleach to make it safe for drinking. That was almost ten years ago, and I still remember how bad it tasted."

She turned onto a narrow side road. "We might as well stop here, since it's on the way."

In front of them was a gravel parking lot with a small green lake behind it. No one was around, either on the beach or in the water. A plywood shack with "SNACKS" painted on one wall was padlocked shut.

"We used to come here to swim," she said, parking the car. "Most people went to the bigger lakes where they could have boats, but this was a good place for kids."

Alex pointed at a discolored white raft floating about forty feet from the shore. "Did you swim out there?"

"Never. I used to think that thing was about two miles out in the water. I didn't learn to swim till I was eight and was never any good at it. Most of my friends couldn't swim at all. There aren't any pools in town, and the big lakes are freezing cold even in summer."

"Did you teach yourself?"

"No. Mummy thought knowing how to swim was important, so she dragged me out here and taught me herself. She had a bright pink swim cap covered in rubber flowers and a funny black swimsuit. I was so embarrassed by her outfit, and so afraid of the water, that I hid in the woods whenever she said we were coming here. Still, I'm glad I finally learned. My brother Jack can't swim a stroke. Mummy couldn't teach him and Daddy said she was wrong, that knowing how to swim wasn't important. He said being able to swim a few feet wasn't going to save anyone who fell in the icy water around here and swimming for fun was for lazy rich people who didn't get enough exercise working."

Alex looked at her in silence for a minute, then said, "Everyone at my college had to pass a swim test in order to graduate. I have no idea why."

"It's a good thing our high school didn't have that requirement," Willow laughed. "Hardly anyone would have graduated."

"Let's go see the movie theater," she said, starting the engine. "It's the only one in town, except for the drive-in. It's sort of Art Deco, even though it was built in the late forties."

It was too early in the day for the theater to be open, so they pressed their faces against the glass doors and looked into the dim, thickly carpeted lobby. "It's too bad you can't see the upper level from here," Willow said. "The mirrors and light fixtures are really glamorous. When I was a kid, I'd walk up and down that curved staircase very slowly and imagine I was wearing an ice blue, satin evening gown." She turned away from the doors. "It's a shame we can't go in, but you'll see it one of these days."

"Have you ever been to the Savoy or Claridge's in London?" Alex asked.

"I've walked by, but never been inside. Why?"

"I was just thinking you'd like them, if you like Art Deco. I could take you to tea at one of them when I see you in London in December."

They drove by the library, town hall, and post office before pulling up in front of a long, single-story, flat-roofed building. It was a drab structure, painted a gloomy grayish green color, with weeds sprouting up through cracks in the asphalt parking lot. "This is where I went to school through sixth grade," Willow said, getting out of the car.

"How depressing," Alex remarked, closing the car door behind him. "Was it awful?"

She looked at him in surprise. "No, not at all. It was wonderful. I have good memories from those years."

"I'm sorry. It looks so forlorn."

"I guess it does, in a way. The weather is hard on buildings here. And a lot of them were built in a hurry on a tight budget. Come on. I want to show you something out back."

"Is this supposed to be the playground?" he asked incredulously, staring at a flat, empty clearing and a low, dirt-covered hill in back of the school.

She walked ahead of him, her long blond braid swinging from side to side across her back. "I know it looks like nothing, but try to picture it in the middle of winter. Imagine an oval skating rink here, with bright lights on poles and music speakers set up near the ice, and that hill over there covered in snow. Our principal thought everyone should skate every day, so he came out here when the weather got cold and used the fire hose to turn this whole area into a rink. It was magical."

"How did you all learn to skate? Were there lessons?"

She smiled. "No. We just fell down until we got the hang of it." They walked slowly across the clearing. "The big event of the winter was the ice show. Each class had to come up with a routine that included everyone. The parents stood around the rink and clapped, and the cafeteria ladies made the most delicious cinnamon rolls."

She stopped and looked back at the building. "I wish I had their recipe. A lot of people I know would love to have it. But they're all gone now—the principal, the ladies who roasted turkeys and baked rolls from scratch in the cafeteria, the school nurse who wore a starched white uniform with a little hat. Schools are different."

"Do you still like skating?"

Willow began walking toward the end of the building. "I don't know. I haven't had a pair of skates on my feet since sixth grade. My parents wouldn't pay for them after that."

As they came back to the parking lot in front, she added, "You know, the principal always made sure there were skates for everyone whose parents couldn't afford them. I don't know how he did it, but he managed to find dozens of pairs of used skates in different sizes and put them out in the hall for anyone to use. A lot of my classmates were from poor families, much poorer than mine. We were a raggedy-looking bunch, but no one cared." *Except for Jeff's twin sisters and their mother, Carole*, she thought to herself.

Alex was silent, looking at the shabby old building. She glanced sideways at him and it occurred to her that he had probably never gone to a school where anyone was poor or looked raggedy.

"Is the high school nearby?" he asked, looking at her.

"Not far. It has a nice little theater for plays and concerts, but that's the only special thing about it. It wasn't as friendly as this place. The junior high wasn't either." She paused with her hand on the car door handle. "A lot of friendly little kids turn into unfriendly teens, don't they? And then a lot of them turn nice again later on."

"I don't know," he answered. "I never really thought about it before."

They got in the car and Willow turned to look at him. "I need to get back to work. If I don't get in enough hours this summer, I won't be able to pay for my last term at art school. And if I don't finish, I'll be mad at myself and my mother will never stop telling me I threw away my one chance to get out of here."

Alex leaned back in his seat and looked at her. "How badly do you want to get out of here?"

"I don't, but my mother refuses to believe me. She says I'll change my mind when I'm older and be miserable if I stay here. She says no one makes good decisions when they're young and imagine they're in love."

"Are you really in love, then?" Alex asked. "I've never been in love."

"Mummy says I can't be, that it's not possible at my age, but I think she's wrong."

"How do you know she's wrong? When I was teaching in Seattle, I had students who thought they were in love. They'd spend a lot of time holding hands and kissing in the halls, but it never lasted very long and usually ended in a lot of name-calling, tears, and bad grades."

Willow looked away from him. "I knew kids like that too, but I also know people who fell in love when they were young and it was real and it lasted. People like Artie and Maureen down at the cannery. That's what I want, and that's what I've got with Jeff." She turned the key in the ignition and put the car in reverse. "That's why I've got to finish my program. I have to show my mother that even though I went away and did what she wanted, I still could come back and be happy here."

"I'm sure she just wants what she thinks is best for you."

"She wants what would have been best for her. You see, during the war she fell in love with an American stranger, my father, and got married almost overnight, then left home, which for her was England, forever, and it was all a big mistake. I know she respects my dad and I think she even loves him in a way, but she hates it here and never should have left home. Now she wants me to do the same thing in reverse and find some English stranger over there to marry, but I can't live the life she thinks she should have had."

A cold gust of wind blew through the car. Alex began cranking his window shut. "How much vacation do you have before your classes start?"

"None. I'll take a few days off at the end of the season to help my parents get ready for winter, then go to London just a day or two before school begins." She backed the car out of the parking lot. "Most people here don't even know what summer vacation is. There's too much work to do before everything freezes up. Your students are going to be working, either at paying jobs or helping their parents, right up until the first day of school."

"I was going to have them write an essay about their summer vacations. That's how I always started the year at my old job."

"I wouldn't do that. Have them write about something that happened at work or about getting ready for winter."

She turned onto the main road. Alex looked at his watch. "Can I buy you lunch?"

"You don't need to."

"Please. Your mother and you have been so kind to me. It's the least I can do. And I have to eat before I go over to the high school."

She wasn't hungry and wanted to get back to work. "Okay, but it has to be quick. There's a place near here that makes good fish and chips."

"That sounds great."

They sat at a picnic table outside the restaurant. Willow ate a few fries and drank a Coke, explaining that she'd lost her taste for fish when she started working at the cannery, while Alex wolfed down the fried halibut. She had a feeling he hadn't been eating very well since he got to town.

"Is this your first time living on your own?" she asked.

He stopped chewing and looked up. "Yes. Except when I lived in the dorm at college or was away at summer camp."

"Maybe you should talk to Keith's wife about eating with them. I don't think she'd charge very much."

"I guess I could do that, but I was going to try cooking for myself."

"Did your mother teach you how?"

"No. She's old-fashioned. She doesn't think men belong in the kitchen."

"I see. Well, talk to Keith's wife. She's a good cook."

When they had finished, she drove back down to the cannery and left Alex at the gate. He waved goodbye as she ran to the office.

Jeff looked up from his desk, smiling slightly when she came in. "Hey, Babe. Sammy says you ran off with a stranger in a flashy car."

"The car was Keith's old station wagon. And the stranger was that teacher from Seattle, the one Mummy had to tea. I think he felt obligated to take me out to lunch. And he wanted some tips on how not to seem like an outsider."

"Did you tell him that's impossible?"

"Sort of, but it doesn't matter. He only wants to stay here long enough to get some ideas for a book. I'll be amazed if he makes it to the end of the school year." She ran up the stairs to the apartment, saying, "I've got to change and get back to work."

When she came back down, Jeff was still at his desk. She kissed him quickly as she ran by, saying, "You hardly slept at all last night. Let's go to bed early."

He watched as she ran out the door. She was right; he was exhausted. He didn't want to see Paul, but rumors about what he had done were getting around. Eventually, Willow's father and brother would hear about it and there'd be trouble. Jim had an ugly temper and Jack did whatever Jim told him to do. It was easier for him that way. Paul had to get out of town.

That evening, Jeff heard John trudging slowly up the stairs to their apartment. He knew John hated visiting them there. One January night when he'd stopped by after drinking too much bourbon, John had broken down and told him he couldn't stand the sight of their old brass bed and rumpled quilts through the open bedroom door, that he hated the way they squished together, thigh to thigh and shoulder to shoulder, on the threadbare velvet loveseat in the living room. He said being at their place reminded him too much of his life before his wife left, and seeing it felt like a punch to the gut.

Jeff opened the door and handed him a mug of hot Russian tea. He wasn't going to give John a drink, even if he asked for it. There probably wasn't any booze in the apartment anyway. Willow didn't drink at all, and he only had a beer now and then when they went out.

They had all grown up knowing plenty of people with drinking problems, people who sent their kids to school inadequately dressed with no breakfast. That was why the grade school principal, a practical man, kept a box of old winter clothes in the hall outside his office. Some of their best friends had needed to paw through that box on a regular basis. The ones who were too embarrassed to do it got frostbite.

"Thanks for coming," he said. "I know you'd rather be at home."

"What's up?" John sat down in his usual spot, facing the two of them.

"The hospital says they're discharging Paul at the end of the week. They want to know who's going to pick him up and get his medicine."

"Is he coming back here?"

"No. I don't want him on the property and I don't want Willow to see him. I don't want to see him either, but I have to. I've got to fire him myself, not leave it to someone else. We've gotta come up with a plan."

"He's got a sister in Oregon. He should go there."

"Can you call her and tell her what's going on, at least the part about him being in the hospital? Not the part about him and Willow."

"Yeah." John set his half-empty mug on a low table in front of the loveseat. He hated Russian tea almost as much as Florence did. "I guess he can stay at my place until the medics say he can travel."

"Will he go along with that after what you did to him?"

"I think so. It's not like he's got a lot of choices, right? I don't see anyone else offering to put him up. His buddies are all on the beach gang, and they live here. Anyway, I've been over to see him at the hospital and he feels really bad about what he did. He doesn't even remember most of it." John glanced at Willow, who was staring into her tea with a faraway look on her face. "Sorry to bring it up again," he said.

"What? Oh, that's okay. I'm pretty tired."

Jeff put his arm around her shoulders.

John looked away for a moment, then back at Jeff. "Are you gonna come out to my place and tell him he's fired and can't hang around town? What makes you think he'll listen? You can't make him leave."

"I'm hoping his sister can talk him into leaving. And I'm gonna make it clear that things will only get worse for him if he stays. If I don't break down and go after him myself, then Willow's dad and brother will for sure, once they get wind of this."

John stood up. "All right. I'll get hold of the sister and make up a bed for him at my place. I should get going."

After John had gone, scrambling down the stairs as if he couldn't stand another second in their apartment, Jeff went down to lock the office door. It was late, but still light outside. The days were getting shorter as the season came to an end. It wouldn't be long before termination dust, the first snow on the lower mountains, signaled the end of the summer jobs. Miss Vinnie, Sylvester, and a lot of the other outsiders would pack up their belongings and head for the highway leading to Canada and the lower forty-eight. He would drive Willow to the airport and send her on her way to Anchorage, where she would catch a plane to London. The cannery, slime house, and bunkhouse would be scrubbed clean and locked up. Sammy would fly to Arizona to spend the winter with his sister. Alone in the apartment, Jeff would play Willow's favorite record albums on the stereo and climb into their bed alone, wrapping his arms around her pillow, which always smelled slightly of roses.

CHAPTER 8

"Looks like you'll be leaving us today, Mr. Mitchell," the stocky, middle-aged nurse said as she pushed a rolling cart into Paul's hospital room on Thursday morning. He was sitting up in bed and had just finished breakfast. His left hand was bandaged and the bruise on his cheek had faded to yellow. "I'm going to remove your IV, then we'll get you dressed. One of your friends dropped off some clean clothes."

Paul scowled and pushed his tray table away. "I don't have any friends." He looked out the window at the gray clouds and scrubby spruce trees while she bustled around the room. There seemed to be a hole in his memory that stretched from Saturday night to Tuesday morning. That was when he woke up to find John hanging over his hospital bed asking, "How ya feeling, buddy?"

The nurse opened a paper bag and pulled out a neatly folded bundle of clean clothes. "See? They even put a card in here." She handed him a pale blue envelope with his name written on it in tidy Palmer script.

He ripped it open and pulled out a card with a picture of flowers and a puppy on the front. Inside, beneath the printed message, were the words "Best wishes for a good recovery, Lavinia and Sylvester."

"Throw them in the trash," he said, holding the card and envelope out to the nurse.

She took them, frowning. "Why do you want to do that?"

"I don't need that crap. It's for kids. And women." Tossing the blanket off, Paul swung his legs over the side of the bed and tried to stand up.

"Where do you think you're going?" she barked. "You've still got that IV in your arm, young man. Get back in bed now."

An hour later, a grim-faced orderly pushed him across the lobby in a wheelchair. They waited by the glass entrance doors, Paul clutching a wad of crumpled discharge papers and a bag of dirty clothes on his lap. When John's truck pulled into the patient loading zone, the orderly wheeled Paul out, hoisted him into the passenger seat, and slammed the door shut without saying a word.

"Not a very friendly guy," John remarked, watching him push the empty chair back inside.

"I wasn't very nice to him this week," Paul muttered. "Wasn't very nice to anyone."

"They saved your life."

"Yeah, I know. That's what everyone keeps telling me."

"It's true. Starting with Jeff."

"Good old Jeff. Always the hero. No wonder he gets the beautiful princess."

"Knock it off, Paul."

"Hey, we gotta stop at a pharmacy. There's some stuff I'm supposed to get."

John turned the key in the ignition. "I'll get it later, after I drop you off."

Paul yawned and stretched his legs. It felt good to be out of bed. "I hope Dan hasn't been using my room. He's always had his eye on it."

"We aren't going down there. We're going to my place."

"Why's that?"

"You gotta rest. The bunkhouse is no good for that."

"That Jeff's idea?"

"Yeah. And mine." John turned onto the road leading out of town and pressed the accelerator.

Paul watched him for a few moments in silence. "Bullshit. You all told him about Saturday night, didn't you? I thought you weren't gonna tell him, but you did."

"Let's not talk about it now. He's coming over later."

"Why? What's he gonna do? Beat me up? Put me back in the hospital?"

"Jeff isn't like that."

"How do you know? You never got drunk and grabbed his girl-friend."

"Just shut up, Paul. You look like hell."

"I thought you were my friend, John. I didn't even mind that you had to pound on me a little when I was acting crazy. I shoulda known better."

"I am your friend."

"Maybe, but you're his friend first. And hers. I'm just an out-sider, nothing but a damn outsider."

They drove on in silence, Paul staring out the side window, his bandaged hand resting on his knee, until he finally dozed off.

John lived ten miles out of town on a couple of acres next to a creek. He was always working on his house, an old Quonset hut, adding little rooms and windows in odd places. The clearing around it looked like a campground, with canvas tents pitched here and there and a tarp-covered outdoor kitchen over to one side. A small travel trailer, the summer home of Nancy and her girl-friend Jane, sat next to a dilapidated shed where she kept her motorcycle. No one was around. They were all down at the cannery.

The truck bounced up a rutted dirt road and came to a stop near the front door. Paul was still asleep, his head flopped back and his mouth hanging open.

John reached over and shook his shoulder. "Hey, wake up. You can go back to sleep once we get inside."

"What?" Paul opened his eyes and looked around.

"We're here. Can you get out by yourself?"

"Yeah. There's nothin' wrong with my legs."

"Good. How's that foot? You were limping on Sunday."

"It's okay." Paul opened the truck door with his right hand and climbed out. "They just make you sit in that wheelchair cuz they're afraid of getting sued."

They went inside and John pointed toward the back of the building. "You can stay in the extra room, down there on the right. You know where the bathroom is."

"Okay, but I still don't see why I can't go back to my own room."

John looked at his watch. "I've gotta get back to work. Help yourself to whatever's in the fridge. And remember, the doc said no booze."

"I'm just gonna rest for a while," Paul said, grimacing as he eased himself into a worn leather armchair.

"All right. I gotta run. I left Nancy in charge and she's got a short fuse."

"Tell her I can still feel that right hook."

"I will. Try to get some sleep. They said it's the best thing for you."

When John walked into the warehouse a little before noon, he heard Nancy bellowing over the sound of the forklift. "I told you not to get under the load, you idiot! You want to leave that kid of yours with no father?"

He walked around a stack of boxes just in time to see Kenny jump out from under the raised forks. "What the hell's going on here?" he shouted.

Nancy lowered the load, shut the forklift off, and jumped down from her seat. "That moron ran under the load. I don't know why. Ask him." They both looked at Kenny.

"There was a piece of rope caught between the forks and the load. I was trying to pull it off so it wouldn't get caught on anything."

"Don't let me catch you doing anything that stupid again," John said. "Go open the cooker."

He turned to Nancy. "Paul's at my place. He says he can still feel that right hook you gave him."

"Good. He had it coming." She clambered back on the forklift and turned the key in the ignition. "What are you gonna do with him?"

"Let him rest for a few days, then get him out of town before Jim Marsh gets back and hears about it."

"Where is he?" she asked, raising the forks a few inches off the floor and shifting into reverse.

"He and Jack took a bunch of guys from California out fishing."

"Jim won't do anything. He doesn't give a damn about Willow."

"Maybe, but he'll blow up when he hears what the regulars at the Snowshoe are saying about him, that he's too old to go after Paul."

"I don't know how that miserable wife of his puts up with him. I hear she's nuts, pretends she's still in England all the time."

As the forklift backed away, John turned and saw Jeff walking toward him across the warehouse floor.

"You got Paul yet," Jeff asked.

"Yeah, he's at my place, feeling sorry for himself as usual."

"Did you get hold of his sister?"

"Yeah. She'll be here tomorrow night. She didn't want to get involved, but I talked her into it. Sounds like he's been a problem for the family ever since he got back from 'Nam."

"Well, he isn't gonna be our problem any longer. I'll come out to your place tonight, and we'll tell him what's going on." Jeff paused, watching Kenny drag gondolas out of the cooker. "The end of this lousy season can't come soon enough for me," he said bitterly.

John looked at him in surprise. "You shouldn't say that. We need every day of work we can get. You're just mad at yourself for not firing Paul and Lavinia years ago. Don't worry. Winter will be here soon enough, and you'll be sitting in my kitchen wishing it was summer and the tanks were full of fish."

"Yeah. You're right. I just can't stop griping, can I?" Jeff smiled. "All right. Thanks for everything. I can't stop blaming myself for not being in the slime house that night."

"You can't be everywhere. It happened and it's over. Let's get that loser out of town and forget about him."

"I hope Willow can forget him."

John thought for a minute. "I think she'll be okay," he said at last. "She would've sliced him to pieces with that knife of hers if he'd tried to do more than grab her. He's just a pathetic creep, not a criminal. I could tell by the look on her face when he started blubbering that she was gonna be okay."

"We'll see," said Jeff. "I wish she wasn't so damn stubborn about working late. She should never have been alone in there. From now on, I'm going to make sure Mike is always the last one to leave. No more sneaking off early to go dancing." Jeff turned to go. "Okay, see you later."

"I'll be taking off at five. I gotta pick up some medicine for Paul. He needs a dose at six."

"You're a good guy, John. I'll tell Sammy to pack up some supper for you and Paul. Come over to the bunkhouse and get it before you go."

Chapter 9

Paul opened his eyes suddenly. He was shaking all over and felt rivulets of sweat trickling down his face. His right hand, the one that wasn't bandaged, was clenched in a tight fist. Slowly, he became aware that a persistent knocking sound, which, in his dream, had been a chopper overhead in Viet Nam, was actually the sound of someone pounding on the front door.

"Hold your horses! I'm coming!" he shouted. He rolled over and pushed himself out of the waterbed in John's extra room. He had gone in there for a nap, but the sloshing sounds and bad dreams just made him feel worse.

He walked slowly through the house, still limping a bit, and pulled the door open. Outside, Sylvester was standing on a rubber mat that had been thrown down over the dirt. His hair, what little there was of it, was slicked down across the top of his head in an unsuccessful attempt to hide a large bald spot. His burgundy knit golf shirt stretched tightly over his pot belly.

"Hi there. How ya feelin'?" he asked in a cheerful voice that set Paul's teeth on edge. "The missus said you was out of the hospital, so's I thought I'd stop by and see how you was doin'."

"I'm all right, no thanks to that wife of yours." Paul stood in the doorway, rubbing his eyes and wiping the sweat off his face with his sleeve. He had no intention of inviting Sylvester inside, even if he had just driven all this way to check on him.

"That's an awful big bandage you got on your hand there. How long you gotta keep it on?"

"Dunno. A while." Paul started to close the door.

"Whoa. Just a minute, buddy. I come out here to take you into town for a beer. I'm buying."

"I'm not supposed to be drinking. Doc said no booze."

"A coupla beers ain't drinkin'. You know that. Go get your boots on."

"What time is it?"

"Just a little after two. Come on. You look like you need cheering up."

Paul thought for a minute. No one would be back at John's before six and he didn't want to spend the whole afternoon alone. He'd already looked through John's records, but there weren't any he liked. There were a bunch of books on a shelf, but no westerns or war stories. Just old history stuff and sissy poetry. "Okay. Wait here," he said at last.

At the Snowshoe, seated on two red leatherette stools at the far end of the bar, they pretty much had the place to themselves. Setting his beer glass down, Paul turned to look at Sylvester. "You know your old lady is the reason I got my hand all messed up like this, right?"

"Now that ain't right, son. She never told you to go pushin' yourself on that girl like an animal. Don't you know anything about women?" Sylvester wiped beer foam off his mouth with the back of his hand. "Hey, Bob. You got any pretzels?" he called out to the bartender, who was polishing glasses at the other end of the bar. "Anyways, I hear it was fish poisoning and brandy that made you so sick. You can't blame Lavinia for that."

"She told me she knew for sure that Willow wanted me to make a move. Why'd she set me up like that? I never did anything to her."

"You didn't 'make a move,' son. Everyone says you went after that girl like a wild dog." Sylvester shoved a handful of pretzels in his mouth. "You're lucky she only cut your hand. She mighta done worse." He laughed. "You ever seen her slice through a salmon with that knife of hers?"

"I wasn't gonna do anything bad to her. I love her." Paul drained his glass.

"Nice way to show it." Sylvester waved at the bartender. "How about another round, Bob?"

"Bet she won't even say hi to me in the bunkhouse."

"Prob'ly not."

"Maybe if I apologize and tell her I wasn't thinking straight."

Sylvester raised a fresh glass to his mouth and took a big swallow. "Can't hurt. Women like it when men apologize."

"Maybe I should get her a present."

"Women like that too. Now you're thinking. How about a little tequila?"

Jeff pulled into the parking lot on the side of the Snowshoe at about four. He waited in his truck for a few minutes, then climbed out and went inside. When Bob had called to tell him Sylvester and Paul were over there getting loaded, his first thought was to do nothing. After all, he didn't give a rat's ass about either of them, so he went back to the paperwork on his desk, but the rage building up in his head wouldn't go away.

Bob looked at him from behind the bar and nodded toward the two stools at the far end. There were only a half dozen customers in the place, so it was easy to spot them. Walking quietly up behind Paul, Jeff grabbed the back of his shirt collar and jerked him backward onto the floor, where he lay, stunned, holding his bandaged left hand and moaning. He put his heavy work boot on Paul's chest and looked down at him. "That was for Willow." He kicked him in the ribs. "And that's for me." Paul rolled onto his side, gasping for air.

No one said a word. Sylvester was silent, sitting pop-eyed on his stool.

Paul propped himself up on one elbow, coughing. "What the hell?"

Jeff looked down at him. "I was gonna tell you tonight, but I'm telling you now. You're fired, and your sister's coming to get you tomorrow. If you don't get your ass out of town, Jim and Jack Marsh will make you wish you'd never heard of Alaska."

"Now go easy on him, son. He ain't feeling good on account of being so sick." Sylvester hopped down from his perch and helped Paul get up off the floor. "This ain't like you, Jeff."

Jeff felt the anger that had overwhelmed him begin to fade away. Paul slumped down in a chair that someone had pulled over from a nearby table and put his head in his hands.

"I been working for you, and your granddad before you, for years," he said, "and this is the first time I ever got really out of line."

"That's true," Sylvester said, handing Paul a glass of water that Bob had shoved across the bar. "He's got a good point there, Jeff." Paul took a few sips.

"You can't stay here. Go home with your sister and get straightened out."

"She don't want me hanging around her place. Nobody does."

"I know you had a rough time in Viet Nam, but you're not getting any better here. Look at you. Down here getting drunk when you just got out of the hospital this morning."

"That's Sylvester's fault."

"Don't blame me! I was just tryin' to cheer you up." Sylvester looked up at Jeff and shrugged his shoulders.

Jeff put his hand on Paul's shoulder. "I'm sorry it had to end like this. You did a good job running the beach gang, but I never should have let you get away with all the other shit." He looked at Sylvester. "Are you sober enough to drive him back to John's place?"

"'Course I am. Steady as a rock."

"Then do it. And don't think I don't know about Lavinia and her part in all this."

"She didn't make him go crazy."

"No, but this time she went too far with her troublemaking. You keep your complicated love life out of my cannery, unless you want her to get fired next."

After Jeff had gone back to his truck, Paul finished the glass of water and stood up. "I'm not going to John's place now," he said, rubbing his sore ribs. "I gotta walk around for a while and do some thinking. I'll hitch a ride out there later."

Sylvester started to get off his stool. "I brung you here and I'm taking you back. I'm real sorry about all this."

"Stay here and have another beer, Sylvester. And leave me alone. I'm not a baby."

Paul stood on the sidewalk outside the Snowshoe, lost in thought, then turned left and began walking. A few blocks down the street, he came to Maggie's, the local secondhand store. The plate glass window facing the street was grimy inside and out. A garland of holly and some snowflakes, spray-painted on the window last Christmas and never washed off, looked depressing in the gray summer light. A dead cactus in a yellow ceramic pot sat in the window, along with stacks of old magazines and broken toys. Two bald mannequins wearing used clothes stared out at the sidewalk like lost souls beckoning to other lost souls. Paul pushed the door open, making a string of bells on the inside doorknob jingle loudly.

Everyone in the store looked his way. He waved his bandaged hand at them.

The store was lit by a couple of fluorescent fixtures mounted to the ceiling and smelled of dirty clothes, mildewed books, and old popcorn. A popcorn cart and a gumball machine stood next to the counter. The owners, Maggie and Stan, sat in matching armchairs behind the register. They sold a lot of gumballs to bored children who nagged their parents for a nickel, but the stale popcorn sat untouched, day after day, week after week.

Paul greeted them as he made his way to the back of the store. "Hey, Mags. Stan. How's business?"

Maggie, a heavily made-up woman in her fifties with dyed black hair and large hoop earrings, answered, "Could be better." Paul had heard rumors that she had worked in a brothel in her younger days, but he didn't believe them. She seemed too domestic and motherly to him, always knitting or crocheting something or fussing over Stan. On the other hand, her figure was still strikingly voluptuous. He could picture her as a very alluring young woman.

Stan, her rail-thin husband, asked, "Whatsa matter with your hand, Paul? Fight?"

"Yeah."

"Aren't you getting too old for that?"

"I sure as hell am. Hey, you got any new records? I'm looking for something particular."

Maggie waved her arm toward the back of the store. "Go take a look. Some girls brought in a bunch last week. They were leaving town and needed cash."

"I'd never sell my records, if I had any."

He sat down on an overturned plastic crate and began methodically going through the cardboard boxes full of record albums that were scattered across the concrete floor. He flipped through a box of Christmas albums—Ray Conniff, Percy Faith, the Mormon Tabernacle Choir—followed by a box of nothing but Tijuana Brass and Andy Williams. Another box was all film soundtracks. *Sound of Music*, *South Pacific*, *Dr. Zhivago*, and dozens of others. He paused briefly, pulling out the soundtrack from Zeffirelli's film of *Romeo and Juliet*. The picture of Olivia Hussey and Leonard Whiting on the cover brought tears to his eyes, which he quickly wiped away. He had seen that movie at least five times when it came out in 1968, always alone.

At last he found the record he was searching for, sandwiched between Glen Campbell and Gordon Lightfoot in a box that was a little damp on the bottom. The one he wanted was still dry and in fairly good condition, so he took it up to the register. "How much for this one?"

"How about a buck? That one's not too old."

Paul handed Maggie the money. "Hey, you got any wrapping paper you don't need? I want to give this to someone."

"We got some plain brown stuff, but don't you want something nicer than that? There's a store across the street that sells pretty paper."

"Nah, brown paper is good enough. Can I borrow a pen and take one of these business cards?"

Stan pushed a pen across the counter. "Go ahead. The paper's in that box by the back door. You better take the Scotch tape with you. Bring it back when you're done."

Paul fished a piece of paper out of the box, then sat down to write a note on the back of the business card. He taped the card to the album cover, then wrapped it all up in brown paper. On the outside he wrote "Willow Marsh."

Chapter 10

When the whistle blew at five o'clock, Willow got cleaned up and went outside with the other slimers. It had been a long day and there were still a lot of fish to can before they could shut down for the night. Sammy, who was watching for her from the bunkhouse kitchen, hurried over with a small bundle wrapped in paper towels.

"What's this?" she asked, taking it from him.

"It's a maple bar. There was only one of 'em in the doughnut order this morning, and I wasn't gonna let those beach gang bums get their grubby hands on it, so I put it away for you. I meant to give it to you at morning break."

"Thanks, Sammy. That's really nice. I'd give you a hug, but then you'd smell like fish." She put it in her sweatshirt pocket. "I'm going to save it for later. Do you know where Jeff is?"

"Yeah, he's in the office. He went over to the Snowshoe and fired Paul this afternoon. Roughed him up a bit too, from what I hear."

"That doesn't sound good."

"Well, the crazy bastard had to go. Best to get it over with. Now Dan can have his room and his job."

The sound of tires crunching on gravel made them turn and look toward the gate where a mud-spattered pickup with a missing headlight and a dented fender was just pulling up. A young man wearing a stained gray t-shirt and ripped jeans opened the door and got out. His long, dark brown hair was pulled back in a messy ponytail. "Hey!" he shouted in their direction. "You all know a chick named Willow Marsh? I got somethin' for her." He reached in the cab of his truck and pulled out a package wrapped in brown paper.

Willow walked over to him. "I'm Willow Marsh. What is it?"

"Dunno. A guy in Maggie's gave me five bucks to drive it down here." He handed it to her. "It's got your name on it."

"Who gave it to you?"

"Dunno. Just some guy. He had a big ol' bandage on his hand."

He climbed back in the truck, slammed the door shut, and rolled the window down. "Say," he said, leaning out the window, "you look just like a mermaid. Anyone ever tell you that? You got them green mermaid eyes and that long mermaid hair. When do you get off? You wanna go out tonight?"

Willow looked at him. "You know that guy who gave you this?" She held the package up. "The one with the bandage."

"Yeah."

"I sliced his hand open with my mermaid knife last Saturday, and my boyfriend, King Neptune, beat him up today." She began walking away, then looked back and waved. "Thanks for bringing this down here."

Jeff was waiting for her outside the office. "Who was that?" he asked.

"Some creep. Paul gave him five dollars to bring me this." She showed him the package.

"That's weird. Are you gonna open it now?"

"No. Just put it on your desk. We can open it later."

Jeff took the package. "Feels like a record album to me. Go get something to eat. I'll be over in a few minutes. I need to talk to Dan before they all come in for supper."

Out on the dock, the beach gang was unloading the *Ashley B*. No one was arguing or cracking jokes. They never thought Jeff, easygoing Jeff who put up with all sorts of shit, would really fire Paul, much less knock him around on the day he got out of the hospital.

They were in a hurry to get to the Snowshoe. Dan and Gary were going to get Paul and take him out for one last good time before he had to leave town. It was the least they could do for their old friend. And there was always a chance Jeff might change his mind and let Paul come back if they gave him the silent treatment and some dirty looks.

"Dan!" Jeff shouted over the noise of the forklift. "Come here."

Dan drove over and turned the engine off. "What is it? What's wrong?"

"Listen. I know how you guys feel about Paul. I don't feel good about it either." He took a last swallow of coffee from the paper cup he was holding. "But he went too far this time and you know it."

Dan looked at him from his seat on the forklift. "You know Paul. He wouldn't hurt a fly. He just likes to fool around."

"He wasn't fooling around this time."

"All the girls are used to his bullshit. Just ask them."

"Yeah, I know, but this was different."

"We were all pretty loaded that night. And Paul was sick. He wasn't thinking straight."

Jeff crumpled the empty cup and threw it in a nearby trash can. "I can't let him come back, Dan. His sister is coming up from Oregon. She's gonna take him home."

"Give him a break, man. You know he saw a lot of bad shit over in 'Nam. It kinda screwed him up."

"I know all about that, and I've been giving him breaks, but he's getting worse, not better."

"Did you know he wasn't drafted? His old man made him sign up. Said it would make a man out of him."

"Yeah, I know that too." Jeff shivered in the cold wind blowing across the dock. He had left his jacket in the office. "Well, his father's dead now, so maybe he can straighten himself out. This place isn't doing him any good."

"Me and the boys are gonna take him out for a few beers tonight."

"Leave him alone, Dan. He's still sick and we don't need more trouble."

"The guys'll be sorry they didn't get to say goodbye."

"Yeah, I know."

In the bunkhouse kitchen, Sammy was getting ready to dish up supper. He stirred the big pot of pork and beans that was bubbling on the stove and opened the oven to check on his cornbread. Three apple pies sat on the counter.

"Hi, Sammy, you got some food packed up for me?" John asked as he came through the door. "I gotta run. Paul needs his medicine at six."

"Yeah, everything's ready," Sammy answered, handing him a bulging grocery bag.

Willow came in as John was leaving. "What's going on?" she asked.

"I gotta go home. Paul needs his medicine and I haven't been able to get him on the phone. He's probably asleep."

"Does he know his sister is coming in tonight?"

"Yeah. Jeff told him. Thanks, Sammy. You should open a takeout restaurant."

"Get outta here. And you can tell that bum I ain't gonna miss him."

After supper, Willow and Jeff took the package up to their apartment. They sat down on the old loveseat and looked at it.

"It's kinda strange, isn't it?" Jeff observed. "I mean using plain brown paper like that."

"Yeah." Willow turned it over and started undoing the tape. She pulled out the album, letting the paper fall to the floor. It was a used copy of *Ode to Billie Joe* by Bobbie Gentry, a little faded and water damaged. There was a business card from Maggie's with some writing on it taped to the cover.

"What's it say?" Jeff asked.

Willow read it silently, then handed it to Jeff. He read it out loud.

'Sorry for what I did. You were right to cut me with your knife. Billie Joe did the right thing too. Love, Paul.'

Jeff handed it back to her and stood up. "I need to call John."

"He said he couldn't get Paul on the phone. He said he must be napping, but what if he wasn't?"

She caught hold of his hand and pulled him down. He put his arms around her and stroked her hair, saying softly, "Whatever happens, it's not your fault, Babe. He's a messed-up guy." He pulled an old blanket off the back of the loveseat. "Here, put this around your shoulders. You're shaking."

"I want to come with you."

"No. Just stay here."

Down in the office, Jeff flipped through the Rolodex until he found John's number. He waited impatiently as it rang and rang. He was about to hang up when John answered, sounding out of breath. "Yeah, who is it?"

"It's me, John. I think we've got a problem."

"Yeah. I know."

"What do you mean."

"Paul isn't here and Nancy's motorcycle is gone. I don't know where the hell he is." John paused to catch his breath. "What are you calling about? Is something wrong in the warehouse?"

"No. The warehouse is fine. Listen, Paul paid some guy to bring Willow a copy of that record album *Ode to Billie Joe*, and there was a note with it saying he was sorry and Billie Joe did the right thing."

"What's that supposed to mean?"

"You remember that song, don't you? It's the one about the kid who's in love and jumps off a bridge."

"And his girlfriend's parents act like it's no big deal? Yeah, I remember it now."

"We've gotta find Paul."

"I'll get the truck ready. At least there aren't any bridges around here. And he didn't take any of my guns."

"I'm going over to the Snowshoe. Someone there might know where he went. Then I'll come out to your place, and we'll start looking for him."

"All right. What time does it get dark tonight?"

"Around ten thirty. We got about four hours."

"Okay. I'll be ready when you get here."

Jeff put the phone down and ran next door to the bunkhouse. Sammy was alone in the kitchen, washing the supper dishes and listening to the radio. The beach gang had gone back to work and Artie had never shown up for supper at all.

He turned around when Jeff came in. "What's the matter? You look like you seen a ghost." He turned the water off, dried his hands, and switched the radio off.

"Paul took off on Nancy's motorcycle and no one knows where he is."

"Maybe he just wanted some fresh air. He's been cooped up in that hospital all week."

"I think he went off somewhere to do himself in."

"What makes you think that?"

"I don't have time to explain. I just wanted to tell you I'm going out searching for him."

Sammy unplugged the coffee urn, took his jacket off the back of a chair, and pulled his cap off a hook. "I'm goin' too."

"Okay. Wait in the truck while I run upstairs and tell Willow."

He ran next door and up the stairs to their apartment. Willow was sitting where he had left her. She looked up when he came in. Her pink bandana had fallen off and her hair was hanging loosely around her face. "What are you doing?" she asked.

"Sammy and I are going out to help John look for Paul. No one knows where he is. He took Nancy's motorcycle."

"Can I come with you? Maybe I should talk to him."

"I think he's past the talking stage. I don't want you getting caught in the middle of this."

"Don't let him hurt you."

CHAPTER 11

Willow heard Jeff run down the stairs and slam the office door shut behind him. A few minutes later, she went into the bathroom, splashed cold water on her face, and braided her hair. She put on a tattered, green, army surplus jacket and her hiking boots, and slipped her knife into one of the deep jacket pockets along with her driver's license, keys, and a few dollars. After locking the apartment door, she went down to the office and called Keith, Alex's landlord, who ran the only taxi service in town. No one noticed her leaving to go wait for him outside the gate. Artie might have been wondering why she wasn't at her sink, but she hoped he'd be too busy to think much about it. She stood next to Sammy's car, listening to the muted roar coming from inside the cannery, until she saw Keith turn off the main road.

"Where ya headed?" he asked as she climbed into the back seat.

"Hi, Keith. I need to go home. Do you remember where it is? You know, out past the grade school."

"Yeah, sure. I remember." He turned the cab around and started driving. "I haven't seen you or Jack in a while. How's he doing?"

He and her brother had been good friends but had a falling out after Keith married Tina, Jack's high school sweetheart. That was four years and two babies ago, but they still avoided each other.

"I think he's doing all right. You know Jack; he never says much about himself. He and my dad spend most of the summer out of town nowadays, taking tourists around."

"You still going away for school?"

"Yeah, but I'm almost done. I'll be back for good by Christmas." She wished he'd drive a little faster.

"You go someplace far away, right?"

Willow knew he didn't have any reason to hurry. Nothing was going on at the airport, and no one else was likely to need his taxi this early in the evening. He'd get busy later, when the last flight from Anchorage got in and people at the bars were too drunk to drive themselves home. Not that a lot of them didn't try. That's why he had a tow truck. In the winter, when there weren't many tourists to pick up and drop off, he kept busy with his snow plow. Almost everyone in town was like Keith, doing a lot of different things to make ends meet. He had a radio in the car so Tina could reach him when someone was looking for a ride or a tow, but it was silent now. "Yeah, too far away," she answered. She was finding it hard to pay attention to what he was saying.

"You and Jeff, you gonna get married?"

"I don't know. We haven't talked about it. Our mothers don't like each other or us being together, so that's a problem."

They pulled up in front of her parents' house. Willow got out and handed him the fare. "Thanks. Say 'hi' to Tina for me."

"Will do. And go ahead and get married. Don't wait for your mothers to get on board cuz it prob'ly ain't gonna happen."

Jeff parked his truck outside the Snowshoe. He looked at Sammy and said, "Wait here. I'll be right back."

Both the front and back doors of the bar were propped open. Sounds of a band tuning up drifted outside. Not many people were there that early, mostly friends of the band who were hoping to get some free beers.

"Hi, Eddie. How's it going? Is Bob still here?" Jeff asked, walking up to the bar.

"Hey, Jeff. No, he went home. What's up?"

"I'm trying to find Paul. Got any idea where he is?"

"No, but I heard about what happened today."

"Yeah, well, now I gotta find him. He was with Sy Stout this afternoon. Is Sy still around?"

Eddie looked down the bar at Sylvester's empty stool. "He must've gone to the men's room. He was here a minute ago."

Jeff was waiting for Sy when he came out, wiping his damp hands on his pants and waving at the band as he made his way back to his stool.

"Come outside, Sy. I want to talk to you."

"Whatsa matter? Ain't somethin' wrong with Lavinia is there?" Sylvester asked, looking slightly worried. "She didn't get hurt down at that sweatshop you're runnin', did she?"

Jeff wanted to knock him on his ass right there in front of everyone. "No. She's okay."

Sylvester shrugged and followed Jeff to the door, shouting, "Eddie, don't let anyone sit on my stool! I'm comin' right back."

Out in the parking lot, Jeff gestured to his truck and said, "Get in."

"What's goin' on?" Sylvester laughed. "You kidnapping me?"

"We need your help. We can't find Paul and we think he's gonna hurt himself, if he hasn't already."

He stopped laughing and climbed in, pushing Sammy closer to Jeff on the bench seat. "Now what makes you think that? He didn't seem so down last time I saw him, everything considered."

Jeff backed out of the lot. "When was that? Did he say where he was going?"

"Just a little before five, I reckon. Said he was gonna hitch a ride to John's and take a nap. I said I'd take him, since I was the one that brung him to town in the first place, but he said he'd get back on his own."

They skidded around a corner, sending a spray of gravel flying through the air. Sammy and Sylvester bounced on the seat and put their hands out to brace themselves.

Sammy straightened his cap. "We ain't gonna find Paul if you roll the truck, Jeff. Better slow down. I still don't know why you think that bum's gonna kill himself. Nobody's told me a dang thing."

"I don't know nothin' either," Sylvester added. "He looked pretty pleased with hisself when he left the Snowshoe."

Sammy looked at him. "Why was that?"

"I told him women like presents and he should get one for Jeff's girlfriend since he felt bad about what he done to her, so he went down to Maggie's and got her a record album. Said he sent it down to the cannery, and she'd never forget he gave it to her. He was smilin' when he was tellin' me about it."

Jeff had slowed down, but was still driving over the limit. "There's a song on that album," he said, "about a guy who jumps off a bridge because he's in love with a girl and it isn't working out. Paul wrote a note to Willow saying he was sorry, and the guy in the song did the right thing. And now we don't know where he is."

"Paul ain't gonna jump off no bridge over no female." Sylvester grabbed Sammy's arm as they bounced through a deep pothole. "He ain't that kinda guy."

"I gotta agree with that," Sammy said. "He ain't no Romeo. He's just an ordinary skirt chaser like the rest of them bums."

"I don't think it's just about that." Jeff turned on the windshield wipers; it was starting to drizzle. "It's about everything, his whole screwed up life." They drove on in silence for a couple of miles.

Finally, Sylvester remarked, "Well, I ain't never heard of any bridges 'round here, have you?"

"There's a rickety old thing over the creek, but that ain't nothin'," Sammy answered. "It's only a foot or two above the water and the creek's not very deep. You could prob'ly wade over to the side if you fell in."

Jeff pulled up outside John's house and they all got out. Sylvester looked pale and queasy after the rough ride and a day of drinking.

He headed for some bushes. John was loading things into the back of his truck.

"Any news?" Jeff asked.

"Nothing. I got hold of Nancy and she said her bike had a full tank of gas. She's mad as hell. And you're not gonna like this," he went on. "She says Willow isn't at the cannery and no one knows where she went. Artie was wondering why she didn't come back to work after supper, so he went up to your apartment and banged on the door, but she didn't answer."

"Shit! I told her to stay put. Damn!"

"Hi, Mummy. I need to borrow Jack's truck," Willow said as she came through the front door. "Do you know where the keys are?"

"Now?" Florence looked up from her grandmother's desk, where she was busy writing letters.

"Yes. I'm in a hurry."

"They're in the drawer next to the fridge. There might not be much petrol in it."

"Thanks. I'll bring it back later tonight or tomorrow morning." After all these years, her mother still said "petrol" instead of "gas." It was so annoying.

"Did you see Alex on Tuesday?"

"Yes. I wish you hadn't told him I could leave work to show him around town."

"He's just the sort of young man you ought to be friends with. Good manners, educated, lovely family."

"Oh, for God's sake, Mummy!"

She ran into the kitchen and pulled Jack's keys out of the drawer, then dashed out the back door and over to his truck. The tank was three-quarters full, enough to get her where she was going and back.

At the end of their long driveway, she turned onto the main road, hit the gas, and headed out of town.

"I been thinking, and I got a pretty good idea where he went. And she's prob'ly headed there too."

Jeff and John stopped talking and looked at Sammy. "You think she went out on her own to look for him? Why the hell would she do that?" Jeff felt a knot growing in his stomach and shoved his hands deep in his jeans pockets to keep them from shaking.

"Where do you think they went?" John asked. His voice was calm and low, a sign that he was in a dangerous state of mind. He looked at Jeff. "You got your pistol with you? I've got two rifles, some climbing gear, and some first aid stuff in the truck."

Jeff nodded.

Sylvester walked out of the bushes, wiping his face with a large handkerchief. "What's that you just said about pistols and rifles? You ain't plannin' to shoot the poor sonofabitch, are you?"

"Let's have it, Sammy. Where?" Jeff asked.

"Well, think about it. The only thing around here that's sorta like a bridge is that old rotted trestle out past the mine. They was gonna put some track out there, but it never got finished on account of the mine shutting down. More than one person has jumped, fell, or been pushed off it over the years." He looked at Sylvester. "Some folks say it's haunted."

"I should have thought of that. Let's get going. Sy, you ride with John. Sammy, stay with me."

"Now wait a minute," Sylvester said, looking pale again. "Ain't no reason for me to go on this goose chase. In fact, you didn't need to drag me out here at all. I'm gonna call someone and get a ride back to town." He looked at John. "Can I go inside and use the phone?"

Jeff grabbed his arm. "You're coming with us."

"Let him go, Jeff. He'll only get in the way." John opened his truck door and started to climb in.

"I said, get in the truck with John. You might be the only person who can talk to Paul. I don't know why, but he seems to think you're his friend." Jeff looked at John. "You know how to get there, right?"

"Yeah. It's been a while, but I remember. We used to party out there in high school."

"What makes you think Paul knows about that old trestle?" Jeff asked Sammy once they were back on the road. "It's not a place people tell outsiders about."

Sammy fiddled with the cap that was now in his hands. "Well, one night about three weeks ago Willow came in the kitchen lookin' for cookies to take upstairs, and we got to talking about ghost stories. She said some people think the balcony in the movie theater is haunted, on account of an usherette being strangled by her boyfriend up there back in the fifties. Then I reminded her about the old mine trestle and all the people who fell off it, but she said she'd been out there lots of times and never saw or heard nothin' scarier than a bear."

"So how did Paul find out? She never talks to him about anything."

Sammy looked out the side window. "Well, he was sittin' at the beach gang table finishing up the blueberry pie when we was talking. I didn't think he was listening, but he musta been."

Jeff tightened his grip on the steering wheel and sped up. When Sammy looked at him in alarm, he said, "Don't look at me like that. We've got to get there before her."

After a while, he muttered, "He thinks he's in love with her, but he doesn't know what the word means."

A quick look in the rearview mirror reassured him that John was following close behind.

CHAPTER 12

Willow peered through the rain-streaked windshield as she bumped slowly up the rocky, overgrown road in four-wheel drive. Sharp tree branches and thick bushes scraped Jack's truck and obscured the way ahead. As she climbed higher, the vegetation thinned out, and the surrounding area grew more visible. Mountains rose around her in every direction, and boulders from old landslides lay strewn about among the scrubby, low-growing plants. She swerved to avoid the ones that had come to rest in the middle of the road.

Eventually, the terrain flattened out and the road dead-ended at the edge of a large clearing. A red and black motorcycle, Nancy's Triumph Bonneville, was lying on its side in the middle of it, but she couldn't see Paul anywhere. She stopped and turned the engine off.

Reaching across to the passenger side of the cab, she opened the glove box under the dashboard. Jack usually kept a .22 pistol in there for shooting cans off stumps when he was bored. She pulled it out, wishing it were a .357 or a .44, and checked to make sure it was loaded, then set it down on the seat beside her.

She could see some weathered timbers, the top of the old trestle, on the far side of the clearing. If Paul had climbed out on it and jumped, she wouldn't know unless she went over there and looked down into the ravine. It didn't seem likely he would have hiked up the mountainside or gone to sit behind a boulder, but he might have. She wasn't sure what she was going to say if she found him alive, but she wanted a chance to say something. Picking up the pistol, she opened the door and jumped out of the truck.

"There she is," Jeff said to Sammy as they came up the last hill. "That's Jack's truck."

"And that's Nancy's motorbike," Sammy replied, pointing out the front window. "Bet he ruined it."

Jeff parked next to the empty truck and got out. Looking around, he shouted, "Where the hell is she?"

Climbing out of the truck more slowly, Sammy put on his cap and zipped his jacket. "She musta gone out on the trestle," he said. "That old thing ain't safe."

John, who had fallen behind when they got into the trees down below, pulled up next to them. He and Sylvester got out.

"No sign of her?"

"No. I've been calling her name, but nothing."

"She might not hear with all this wind." John pulled a rifle off the rack in his truck. "Got your pistol?"

"Yeah."

"Let's get going."

"Make yourself useful for once," Sammy said, looking at Sylvester, "and help me with these climbing ropes. We're too old to use 'em, but we can carry 'em over there."

Willow reached the far side of the clearing and went down a set of lichen-covered steps that led to a narrow walkway connecting the trestle to the hillside. Like the trestle, it was made of weathered, gray wood. There were handrails on both sides, but none of it looked very solid.

Gripping both rails, she stepped out onto the old planks. They creaked and flexed beneath her feet. Fighting a wave of vertigo, she looked down at the ground far below. There was no sign of a body on the gravel around the base of the trestle.

A flash of color, a bit of blue and green cloth, caught her eye. Leaning over the rail, she called out, "Paul! Is that you?"

Sticking his head out from behind a thick support post fifty feet below, Paul looked up at her and waved his bandaged hand. There was another good fifty feet between him and the ground, more than enough to kill him if he fell or jumped. He appeared to be holding on to some of the old scaffolding that was left in place when the mine closed and construction stopped.

"Come to watch me jump, Princess?" he shouted.

"Nobody wants that. Climb back up here and go home."

"Ain't got no home to go to. The bunkhouse is my home, and Jeff took it away from me."

Jeff reached the far side of the clearing and looked down. Willow was standing on a couple of flimsy planks suspended over the ravine, holding on to a wobbly handrail and staring at something far below.

"Babe!" he yelled. "Get back over here." He scrambled down the slippery steps. Uncertain that the planks could support both of them, he reached his hand out.

"Paul's down there. I'm trying to talk him into coming back up. There's a sort of ladder that goes all the way to the ground."

"Who's that up there with you, Princess?" Paul shouted from below. "Prince Charming? Did he come to push me if I don't jump?"

Jeff felt a tap on his back and turned around. Sylvester was standing behind him. The wind had blown his carefully arranged hair off the bald spot on top of his head, and his shirt was soaked. He had tied one end of a climbing rope around his pudgy waist in a crazy knot no sailor would recognize.

"Let me handle this," he said. "Take your girlfriend back to the truck, and help Sammy and John hold the other end of this here rope."

"Are you crazy? You can't climb down this thing." Jeff waved him away. "Go back up there and wait."

"You dragged me out to this godforsaken place so's I could talk to him, and that's what I'm gonna do."

Willow looked over at Jeff. Seeing her standing out there over a hundred-foot drop made him sick. "He says he'll come up," she said, "if I go down and meet him halfway."

"No!" Jeff roared. "Tell him I'll come down. Sy, untie that rope and give it to me."

Sylvester stood firm. "No. He's playin' with the both of you, and I gotta stop it. It's gonna get dark soon, and we can't stand out here forever."

Jeff turned to Willow. "Come on, Babe. This isn't working. Get off that thing."

"Okay. Just a sec." She leaned over the handrail again and shouted, "I can't come down there! Come up here and talk to me."

As soon as Willow was safely on solid ground again, Jeff clutched her hand and hurried her up to the clearing. Sylvester followed.

"What's going on?" John asked.

"He's about halfway down the trestle, waving his arms around and talking bullshit. Says he won't come up," Jeff replied.

Sammy, who was still holding a pile of rope in his arms, spoke up. "He ain't gonna jump. He woulda done it already if he really meant to."

"Now listen up," Sylvester said. "If I don't go down there and talk some sense into that boy, either he's gonna get tired and fall or we're gonna be chewin' the fat out here forever. This is just like something that happened when I was in the army. We was in Italy during the war, and one day my buddy got a letter from his sweetheart sayin' she'd gone off and married the local mortician, so he decided he was gonna do away with hisself right then and there. And if it wasn't for me talkin' him out of it, he woulda done it." He began walking back toward the trestle. "You men just hold tight to the other end of the rope."

At sixty-six, Sylvester wasn't as nimble as he had once been. Old injuries and a lifetime of heavy drinking had only made things worse.

He took a few cautious steps out onto the plank walkway, then scurried across to the top of the wood ladder. It seemed to be firmly attached to the trestle supports. His plan was to get close enough to Paul so they could talk, but not too close.

After he had climbed down about thirty feet, forcing himself not to look at the ground far below, he came to a small platform the workers must have used for something long ago; and he decided that was as far as he cared to go. Keeping a death grip on the ladder, he stepped onto the platform, breathing heavily.

Paul was still twenty feet below him, sitting on a beam and looking across the valley. "I know you're up there, Sy," he said in a loud voice. "I can hear you panting like an old bulldog. Mighty nice view tonight."

"Sure is," Sylvester answered. "Be a shame not to see anything like it again, wouldn't it?"

"Dunno. Sometimes when you see something so beautiful, you just decide there's no point in looking around anymore. Nothing will ever be as good as what you already seen."

"There's lots of beautiful things in the world. You ain't been around long enough to see even a small part of 'em."

"I've seen enough bad things. Can't get them out of my head, day or night, no matter where I go."

The wind picked up, making the whole trestle sway and moan. Sylvester was sweating and shivering at the same time. His hands were clammy, and he was beginning to feel light-headed. He sat down and put his head between his knees.

He had lied to everyone, including his wife, about saving his army buddy. And he had repeated the lie so many times, he had almost forgotten the truth. *That's the way it is with lies*, he thought; *they grow a kind of truth of their own after a while.* But now, sitting out there in the wind and the rain, he remembered what had really happened all those years ago in Italy. He had talked and pleaded, argued, joked, and yelled, but it hadn't made any difference. His friend had gone out in the woods that night and shot himself in the head. This time, he was going to make sure it turned out different.

"You still there?"

Sylvester heard Paul calling up at him. He lifted his head, then slowly pulled himself back onto his feet. "Come up here, son. You need to go back where you got people who know you, where you got roots, if you want those bad memories to go away."

"They don't want me."

"That ain't true. Your sister's gonna be here in a couple of hours. What are we gonna tell her if you fall off this damn thing?"

"She won't care. She's been pissed at me ever since I dumped her best friend."

"Now why'd you do that? Didn't you like her?"

"I loved her. But all I wanted to do when I got back from 'Nam was hit the road. That's why I started coming up here every summer."

"What's her name?"

"Wendy."

"What's she look like? Is she skinny with long, blond hair?"

"Yeah," Paul answered.

"Somethin' like Willow Marsh?"

"Guess so. Never really thought about it."

"Did she marry someone else?"

"Don't think so. Don't care."

"Now that's where you're all mixed up. You think you're in love with Willow, but you ain't. She just reminds you of your girl Wendy." Gripping the ladder, Sylvester leaned over and looked down at Paul. "Look at me, son," he called down to him.

Paul stood up. His clothes were drenched and he was shaking uncontrollably. In the fading northern light, his face had no color.

"Now you hold on tight and listen to me for just a minute, then we're gonna get off this cursed thing." Sylvester felt his voice starting to go hoarse from shouting. "Willow is Jeff's girl and that makes sense cuz they been here all their lives and they belong together, just like how I knew Lavinia was the one for me the minute I laid eyes on her when I was sixteen. That's how God arranges things. You'd never be happy if you got that girl away from Jeff. One day you'd start thinkin' 'bout Wendy, the one that was meant for you, and you'd realize you'd made a big mistake."

Paul didn't answer.

"Now, I'm askin' you again. Come up here. It's time for you to go home."

After what felt like an eternity, the others saw Sylvester coming back up the ladder, followed by Paul. Sy had untied the rope from his waist and tied it around Paul's. They crossed the walkway one at a time, then everyone climbed up the steps and into the clearing. Paul fumbled with the rope with his unbandaged hand, but couldn't undo the knot. John stepped forward and untied it.

"Paul's got somethin' he wants to say to you," Sylvester said, looking at Willow.

"I never meant to hurt you, or even scare you," he said in a voice that was barely audible.

No one spoke. Willow felt Jeff's hand tighten around hers.

Finally, Sylvester said, "He's goin' home. He's got a girl down there in Oregon waitin' for him."

"What's her name?" Willow asked.

Paul answered, "Wendy."

"Like the girl in *Peter Pan*."

"Yeah," he said in a low voice, almost a whisper. "I used to tease her about that. She said I was her lost boy."

"Then you need to go back to her and stop being lost."

Late that night, after Paul had been handed off to his sister, and Sylvester had been reunited with his barstool at the Snowshoe, Willow and Jeff climbed into bed, pulled the quilts over their shoulders, and silently wrapped their arms around each other.

Chapter 13

Jeff's mother, Carole Riversen, opened the door of her harvest gold refrigerator, reached in, and gently shook a fluted copper gelatin mold on the middle shelf. Her brow furrowed and a look of consternation crossed her immaculately made-up face. The lemon salad still wasn't firm enough, and the miniature marshmallows had sunk to the bottom. Had she added too much ginger ale or not drained the crushed pineapple sufficiently?

She had spent the past two weeks while her daughters were away furiously redecorating her ranch-style house on Bainbridge Island. Junk haulers had carted away the bright orange shag carpet, and a neighbor had bought the sectional sofa and plexiglass coffee table. She had painted over the hot pink and chartreuse op art design on the living room wall and hired an electrician to install a chandelier that looked like a wagon wheel over her new Colonial maple dining room set. A reproduction painting of a clipper ship in full sail now hung over the mantel where a Peter Max poster had once happily looked out over many a smoky, boozy all-night party, and a demure spinning wheel had replaced a brass and glass bar cart next to the fireplace.

Cozy, Carole thought, plumping a needlepoint pillow. *Cozy, antique, country.* No more pop, op, groovy, or Carnaby Street. The '60s were well and truly over, and it was time for a change. She was going Early American with a vengeance. Her head was filled with thoughts of Windsor chairs, Philadelphia highboys, and grandfather clocks. She coveted a TV cabinet that looked like a farmhouse dry sink.

Still slim, in spite of having given up smoking, and attractive at forty-eight, Carole dreaded the thought of turning fifty and being an unattached widow. She wanted to marry again, but this time she was going to get it right.

When she was twenty-two and Tom Riversen had proposed, she couldn't get to the altar fast enough and couldn't get pregnant fast enough after that. She had already been a bridesmaid eight times and felt like an old maid. Having paid the price for her haste and foolishness—all those dull years in Alaska looking after three children while her tall, blond husband roamed, lied, and cheated—she knew she could do better. *That salad had better firm up.*

If the ferry was running on time, her dinner guests would arrive from Seattle soon. She opened the fridge again and stared longingly at the pitcher of dry martinis. Could she have just a tiny one to steady her nerves? No. Better not. Harry's daughter would surely notice the smell of gin on her breath even if he didn't, and she couldn't take the chance. She hadn't met Donna, but from what Harry had said, she sounded like a nightmare. Overeducated, bossy, always telling her father what to do. Well, Carole had raised twin daughters and was no pushover. She knew how to handle girls, and this one wasn't going to get in her way.

She massaged the beef in its plastic bag of marinade. She had thought about making Soufflé Supreme, a new recipe from a magazine, but had decided against it. Soufflés might be fashionable, but you couldn't trust them. She'd make that another time, a time when she and Harry were dining alone. If things went her way, he wouldn't notice or care if her soufflé was supreme or not.

Instead, she had made one of her most reliable recipes to go with the beef: a casserole of rice, broccoli, and canned mushroom soup. All she had to do was pop it in the oven at the same time as the meat. For dessert, there were cream puffs from a bakery in Winslow.

She pulled a nut-encrusted cheese ball out of the fridge and centered it on a vintage milk glass platter, then carefully surrounded it with crackers. Carrying it into the living room, she swore as she nearly tripped on the edge of a thick, braided rag rug. She wasn't used to wearing clunky platform shoes and long peasant dresses. Her white go-go boots, fishnet stockings, and leather miniskirts had gone to the thrift store in old shopping bags, and it was going to take time to get used to this new wardrobe. How she wanted a martini. And a cigarette.

Carole had met Harry Lewis at an opera fundraiser. A friend had taken her, saying it was a good way to meet the right kind of people. She had never actually seen the end of any opera, as that would have meant missing the last ferry back to the island at night, but what she had seen had been more than enough. All that incomprehensible bellowing in foreign languages gave her a headache.

Of course, she didn't tell Harry that. She told him La Bohème was the saddest, most beautiful thing she had ever heard, upon which he had taken her hand in his and asked if she'd like to go out on his sailboat.

If there was anything Carole hated more than opera, it was sailing, but she had gazed up at his tanned, lined face, thought about his stately brick mansion on Queen Anne Hill, and said that would be absolutely wonderful.

She set the cheese platter down on her new coffee table, an antique trunk she had found at a flea market and had decoupaged with vintage postcards depicting lighthouses, eagles, and American flags. She had never been east of Missoula or south of Boise in her life, but was hoping Harry would feel comfortable in the room and be reminded of Boston, his childhood home. Her best friend had suggested putting a piece of glass on top of an old lobster trap and using that as a coffee table, but Carole had put her foot down, saying it reminded her too much of her deceased father-in-law and his disgusting fish cannery.

She sighed and checked her eyeliner in the entry hall mirror. If only she could get Jeff to sell that awful place and move to Seattle. He would look devastatingly handsome in a good suit from Frederick's. Then she could get busy and find him an acceptable girlfriend, someone stylish and well-connected in Seattle society. What he saw in that odd, artsy tomboy, Willow Marsh, she would never know.

Time to get the beef and the casserole into the oven. Carole rushed back to the kitchen.

The doorbell rang just after she had set the timer, so she dashed back to the front door. She really didn't like these loose, floaty dresses and dangling bead necklaces. Too damn much stuff to get caught on everything and nothing sexy about them, but her daughters had rolled their eyes and made her go shopping when she told them about Harry.

She took a deep breath and opened the door. There on the porch were Harry, smiling, and Donna, not smiling. His tweed jacket, striped tie, khaki pants, and boat shoes made her want to run to her closet for a cashmere sweater and penny loafers. What had she been thinking, allowing Sherrie and Susie to talk her into this fortuneteller getup? Donna wore a plaid skirt, a shapeless navy-blue cardigan, and knee socks. A plaid headband that matched her skirt kept her chin length brown hair away from her face. Carole looked at her in astonishment. She knew Donna was twenty-four, but she looked like a frumpy ten-year-old in that outfit. Trying to find something complimentary to say, she came up empty-handed.

"Harry! And Donna!" she chirped.

Harry smiled and leaned forward to kiss her cheek. Donna handed her a small box.

"How thoughtful. You really shouldn't have. Come in, come in." Carole stepped back and gestured for them to enter.

As Donna followed her father into the house, she said, "It's a box of Frangos."

"My favorites!" Carole cried. "Love them!" Closing the door, she turned to her guests and asked, "How was the ferry? Any trouble finding the house?"

"Not at all," Harry answered. "I spent a lot of time over here on the island when I first moved to Seattle after college. Had an eccentric great-uncle, an old China Hand, who lived here. Fascinating fellow. Left me a wonderful collection of Chinese art when he passed away. You'll see it when you come to the house. The cook he brought back with him made the best food I've ever eaten."

"How interesting!" Carole felt a sickening feeling of panic rising in her chest. What would he think of her jiggly salad and broccoli casserole? And what would she find to say about his art collection? Tomorrow, she would get up early and hurry over to the Seattle Public Library. They must have something there for people who knew nothing about Chinese art.

Donna walked over to the fireplace and took a close look at the painting of the clipper ship. "Look, Dad," she said, "this is a copy of the painting Grandma has in her Back Bay house. Don't you recognize it?" She turned around slowly, scanning the room. "It smells like paint in here. Have you been redecorating?"

"Why, yes. Just freshening things up. Nothing dramatic."

"We don't change things in our houses. Everything has been in the family forever."

"Now that's not entirely true, honey," Harry said. "Grandma had the drawing room furniture reupholstered when I went away to boarding school."

"Yes, but the fabric looked the same as before. She told me there had been green brocade in that room for a hundred years, and there was no reason to do anything different."

What a bore, Carole thought, *always having things the same as they had always been, generation after generation*. When she moved into that mansion of theirs on Queen Anne, she'd shake thing up.

She smiled at Harry. "How about a dry martini? I've got a pitcher in the fridge. Help yourselves to cheese and crackers." With that, she bolted into the kitchen, the long strings of beads around her neck swinging and clicking as she went.

Taking three chilled glasses and the pitcher out of the fridge, she dropped an olive in each glass, filled them, then drank half of hers in one gulp and refilled it. *What an awful child*, she thought. *I wonder if she takes after her mother. No wonder they're divorced.*

Still, they had just met, and Carole was nothing if not an optimist. Perhaps Donna would turn out to be delightful. After all, she had worked for her father for years, and Harry never stopped saying how proud he was of her. He said she knew all about business—money, taxes, investments—things like that. She shuddered and picked up the drinks tray.

"Here we are!" Carole said, handing the drinks around. "Nice and dry. I remember how you like your martinis, Harry."

He took a sip. "Perfect. Couldn't be better if I'd made it myself."

Donna carried hers to a burgundy leather wingback chair, still stiff and shiny from the department store, and dropped into it. *This young lady really ought to take deportment lessons from my daughters*, Carole thought. *She moves like a sack of potatoes with legs.*

"Dad says you want to sell some property in Alaska," Donna said, leaning forward to smear some cheese on a cracker. "That's why we're here, right?"

Carole nearly choked on her olive. She didn't like the way Donna spoke to her father, or the sheepish way Harry looked at his daughter, as if he were a naughty boy who had been caught fibbing to his mother. "Well, it's true that I have some land up there that I'm thinking of selling," she said, "but that's not why we're having dinner together this evening. You see, your father and I have been seeing quite a bit of each other, and he thought it would be nice if you and I met."

Harry chimed in, "That's right, honey. Carole and I are going to be seeing a lot more of each other from now on, and I'd like you to be friends."

"You said this was a business dinner, and we were going to discuss a deal." Donna took a big swallow and set her empty martini glass down.

"Is that the oven timer?" Carole jumped up from an exceedingly uncomfortable, new ladderback chair. "Why don't you go into the dining room? I'll bring everything in."

Donna pulled herself out of the wing chair and marched silently into the dining room. Harry began to follow her, but changed tack and headed for the kitchen, saying, "I'm going to give Carole a hand."

In the kitchen, Carole was coaxing the salad out of its mold with a great sense of relief and triumph. *It really does look lovely*, she thought. *So cheerful and yellow*. Harry came in and watched her place slices of it on small plates.

"I'm sorry," he said. "There are times when she thinks about business a bit too much."

"Oh, I understand," Carole answered, smiling up at him. "I truly do. My son, Jeff, is the same. He never thinks about anything else. Have you told her about our plan?"

"Not all of it." He picked up the tray holding the salads. "This looks delicious. I had no idea you were such a good cook. My ex, Donna's mother, didn't care what she ate and never went near the kitchen." He leaned over and kissed her.

Carole smiled and relaxed. She knew then that everything was going to be fine. She could manage Donna, even if Harry couldn't, and the three of them would bring Jeff around. He'd see what a great opportunity this was and be living in Seattle by Christmas.

CHAPTER 14

Humming to himself, Sammy pulled two raspberry coffeecakes out of the oven and set them on the counter to cool. Every Saturday night he baked something from his mother's battered old recipe box. She had passed away when he was twelve, but he could still hear her speaking to him in Norwegian and smell the sweet, buttery cakes and cookies she had baked for the family.

The soft gurgling of the coffeemaker and the quiet ticking of the big wall clock were the only sounds in the empty kitchen. There was no background roar from the cannery across the way and no thumping coming through the ceiling from the bunkroom upstairs. The beach gang had gone to the Snowshoe, and Sammy was enjoying the peace and quiet. If he was lucky, he'd be sound asleep with his ear plugs in when they came back. In any case, they didn't come in as late or make as much noise now that Paul was gone and Dan was their boss. He poured himself a cup of coffee, cut a piece of coffeecake, and sat down at one of the tables.

Willow and Jeff walked through the deserted cannery, checking to make sure everything was in order. Jeff no longer trusted anyone to make sure she was safe at closing time, even though Paul was gone. He was always waiting for her in the slime house when the last fish came down the conveyor and kept her close when he made his nightly round of the buildings and dock.

John had switched off the hanging overhead lights in the warehouse. Trains of empty gondolas sat on the wide floor, waiting to be filled in the morning. Jeff tightened the handle on a dripping hose near the patch table while Willow picked up a used rubber glove from the floor under the lidder. In the can shop, the overhead racks held rows of gleaming, empty cans. Everything was eerily dim and quiet, as it would be for many months when the season ended in a few weeks.

On the way back to their apartment, they saw Sammy eating alone at a table in the bunkhouse kitchen and stopped to say goodnight.

"Not such a bad day after all," Jeff said, sitting down across from him with a piece of cake. "I thought it would be worse with two boats in, but neither one of them was even half full."

Willow opened the fridge and pulled out a carton of milk. "Want some?" she asked, looking at Jeff.

"Yeah. Thanks, Babe."

"Gettin' to the end," Sammy said. "You can smell it in the air."

"Dan's doing a good job. Better than Paul. I hope he comes back next year."

"Why wouldn't he?" Willow asked, handing Jeff a glass of milk. She sat down next to him.

"He and Gary are trying to get jobs on the Line. They all are. We can't compete with that. No one can."

"I been meaning to ask you something," Sammy said, setting his coffee cup down on the table. "My sister Ada, the one I stay with in Arizona, she just wrote to say she and Joe are movin' to Florida. They got three little great-grandkids down there, and they want to be by them this winter." He paused. "What I'm sayin' is, I got no place to go when we shut down. I was wondering if I could stay on here. I could help look after things, and you wouldn't have to pay me. I'd buy my own food." He looked at Jeff. "You could go over to England for a visit and not have to worry about this place."

Jeff finished his milk. "Sure, you can stay. And I'll pay for the food if you do the cooking for both of us."

Willow smiled. "I've never been able to talk you into visiting me over there."

"I don't know. We'll see." Jeff stood up. He sure as hell wasn't flying all the way to England. Going to Seattle once a year to see his mother and sisters was bad enough. Flying with a friend in a Super Cub was all right, but huge jets crammed with people guzzling booze and puffing on cigarettes made him sick.

They helped Sammy clear the table. As she opened the door to leave, Willow looked back and said, "By the way, Sammy, I meant to tell you that I won't be here for lunch tomorrow. My dad and brother are supposed to get back tonight, and Mother asked me to come home for Sunday lunch."

"You'll be missing my chicken pot pie."

"Can you save me some for supper?"

"Yeah, if I can hide it from them beach bums."

When the whistle blew at noon the next day, Willow hosed off her rubber boots, hung up her apron, and ran to the apartment. There wasn't time for a bath, so she did her best to wipe any traces of fish off her face with a wet towel. She knew she ought to wear a dress to Sunday lunch, but that meant nice shoes and stockings. Her father would have a fit if her shoes weren't polished, and her mother would look depressed if her stockings had a run in them. In the end, she put on embroidered jeans and a white blouse she had trimmed with bits of lace in an attempt to look like the Yardley of London models.

Coming up her parents' driveway in Jeff's truck, she saw her brother Jack inspecting the new scratches on his truck. She parked and walked over to him.

"Hi."

"Hi. How'd this happen? Mum says you borrowed it."

"It's a long story. I'm sorry. I'll pay to get it fixed."

"Nah. You can't afford it. It was already pretty beat up anyway."

"You and Dad were gone a long time."

"Yeah. Some rich guys wanted us to take them all over the place."

"Fishing?"

"A little. Mostly picture-taking and looking for bears." Jack leaned over to take a closer look at the right front fender. "I'll never understand why outsiders want to spend good money to see bears. I'd pay to never see one again in my life."

"Me too."

Just then the sound of a gong reverberated through the still, cool air. Jack looked at Willow. "Why the hell does she do that? Why can't she just shout out the back door like all the other mothers?"

"The fancy people Granny took her to see when she was little lived in places where they banged gongs to tell everyone when to get dressed and eat. And she reads too many British murder mysteries."

"I'm hungry. Let's go eat," Jack said, laughing and heading for the kitchen door.

In the kitchen, Florence pulled a pan of Yorkshire pudding out of the oven. Roast beef, potatoes, and vegetables were already on serving dishes, waiting to be carried to the table. She was using her mother's yellow-and-gold Minton china and had polished the sterling flatware.

"Jack, carry this platter to the table," she said as they came through the back door. "Willow, find your father and tell him lunch is ready. I think he's taking a nap in the bedroom. He was exhausted when they got in last night."

"All right." Willow went down the hall to her parents' room and pushed the door open. Her father was standing in front of the mirror, brushing his gray crew cut hair with a silver brush that Florence had given him one Christmas long ago. It was odd to see him wearing pressed gray dress slacks, a white dress shirt, and a narrow, dark necktie. His black lace up shoes were polished within an inch of their lives. She was more accustomed to seeing him in a Yukon tuxedo with a pair of hip waders and a rifle.

Mummy must have asked him to doll himself up, she thought, feeling bad that she hadn't worn her dress. This would probably be the only time all summer they could be together for Sunday lunch. Some summers it didn't happen at all.

"Hi, Daddy. Mummy says it's time to eat."

"I know. That damn gong of hers woke me up." He finished brushing his hair and walked to the door. "How are you? Slow day at the cannery?"

"No. I worked hard all morning. I just took time off to come home for lunch."

"Well, let's make sure Mother doesn't drag the meal out too long. You might be able to get a few more hours of work in if we hurry her along."

"Isn't this lovely? All of us together." Florence took off her apron, smoothed her dress, and sat down at the table. "I can't remember the last time this happened. Was it Easter? No, Willow wasn't home then. Jeff came over and I baked a ham."

Jim Marsh ran the bone-handled carving knife over the sharpening steel a few times and began carving the roast. "You've outdone yourself, Mother."

"Thank you, dear. And there's apple crumble with custard for pudding," Florence said, smiling.

"My favorite," Jack said, pouring hot, brown gravy over his beef and potatoes.

Jim served himself last, then sat down and picked up his fork. "How's Jeff doing with the business this summer?" he asked, looking at Willow. "Any better than last year?"

"He says it's the first year he wouldn't be ashamed to show a buyer the books, so I guess that's good," she answered, cutting into her Yorkshire pudding. Jack always drowned his in gravy, but she liked it plain and ate it before touching anything else on her plate.

"Jeff's granddad was a nice old geezer, but he didn't have any idea how to manage that place. That's what happens when you get your money from an inheritance like he did. You never learn how to hold on to it. He pissed away most of what he got from his folks looking for gold, then bought that old cannery with the last of it." Jim swallowed a bite of roast beef. "It's a good thing he died when he did, or he'd have gone bankrupt and lost everything."

Florence looked up from her plate. "Such a tragedy, his wife and son dying before him. I'm sure that's what sent him to an early grave."

Jim reached for the gravy. "Tom was even worse with money than his old man. He'd be rolling in dough one month, then stone broke the next. Called himself a businessman, but he was no better than a gambler. That last deal he got into was a loser, and everyone but him knew it. The only smart thing he ever did was load up on life insurance. And buy that land out at the lake."

Jack looked at Willow, then said, "Jeff's not like them. He's good at business and accounting, that kind of stuff. It's a good thing the cannery ended up being his."

Willow said, "Pass the horseradish sauce, please." She spooned some onto her plate. "Carole wants him to sell it so she doesn't have to tell her friends in Seattle that her son owns a fish cannery."

"That woman is such a snob," Florence said, gazing with satisfaction at the portrait of her great-grandmother in its gilded frame. "She has never been anywhere and knows nothing about her ancestors. She has no reason to put on airs the way she does."

Willow helped her mother clear the table and bring in the dessert. "Dad, have you ever thought about getting a new necktie?" she said, setting a jug of custard on the table. "No one wears skinny ties like that anymore. I could bring you one from London."

"Don't waste your money. One tie is all I need and there's nothing wrong with this one. You can bury me in it," Jim replied. "I could count on the fingers of one hand how many times I need to wear a tie every year. The last time I wore it was to Keith Campbell's mother's funeral at the end of April. Remember, Mother?"

"Such a lovely service." Florence scooped apple crumble onto blue and gold Royal Doulton dessert plates. "Such beautiful flowers. They must have cost a fortune." She handed a plate to Jack.

"You should have been there, son," Jim said, pouring custard over his crumble. "It didn't look right, you not being there."

Jack bent his head over his plate and ate in silence.

Willow looked at him. "What happened? I didn't even know she had died."

"No one knows," her mother answered. "Mary had been having bad headaches for a while, and then one night she went to bed and never woke up. Didn't I write to you about it?"

"No. And I just saw Keith Friday night. He was probably wondering why I didn't say anything."

"Where'd you see him?" Jack asked, looking up.

"I needed a taxi to get over here from the cannery."

Jim looked at her, a forkful of apple crumble halfway to his mouth. "You wasted money on a taxi? Why'd you do that?"

"It's a long story. And it was my money." She didn't want to be the one to tell her father about Paul. Besides, it had nothing to do with him.

She looked at Jack. "Why didn't you go to the funeral?"

"I just didn't feel like it."

Florence set her fork down. "I don't blame you, dear. That tramp Tina led you on and then broke your heart when she married Keith."

"Tina's not a tramp, Mum." Jack handed her his plate for a second helping. "And she didn't break my heart. I just didn't want to get married and she did."

"Then why do you still avoid them?" Willow asked.

"I don't know. I just don't like thinking about the two of them together."

"You'll find someone better," Florence said. "I know you will. Plenty of fish in the sea." She folded her linen napkin, set it next to her plate, and stood up.

"Keith was a fool to get married and have children so young. He couldn't afford it then and probably can't afford it now," Jim said, picking up his coffee cup. "Fine meal, Mother. I'm going to read the paper. Jack, put away the gear we brought in last night. Make sure it's all clean and be careful with those new fishing reels. They cost an arm and a leg. I'll check everything later. Willow, you'd better get back down there and see if you can put in a few more hours. There won't be any more work in a few weeks."

"I know, Daddy. I'm going."

"Tell Jeff it's good to hear he's getting that old place on its feet again."

"I will. Mummy, I'm sorry I can't stay and help with the dishes."

"Daddy's right. You need to get back to work. Never mind about the dishes. I'll have them done in no time." Florence sighed and looked at her daughter. "I'm glad Jeff is doing so well, but I wish you'd go out with boys from good families, like Alex, or the boys you meet at school in London."

"I'm too old for boys, Mummy. And I'm not going out with Jeff. I live with him."

"You know what I mean, dear."

Willow didn't reply. She and Jack went out the back door together.

As soon as it closed behind them, Jack said, "The old man is driving me nuts, Sis. Sometimes I just want to punch him or run away. I thought you were an idiot when you moved into that dump with Jeff, but now I'm glad you got away."

Willow stopped and looked at Jack. His green eyes and pale skin were like hers, but his thick, curly, red hair was completely different. They had often wondered which great- or great-great-grandparent had tossed that redhead gene into the pool. Florence and Jim both said they had no idea and that it must have come from someone in the other's family tree. "What happened?" she asked.

"Nothing. I'm just sick of everything. I hate spending all my time out in the sticks with him. He makes me feel like I can't do anything right, and he talks about money all the time."

"He's proud of you, I know he is. But you know Dad; he can never stop worrying, especially about money." She looked into his tired eyes, suddenly noticing that even though he hadn't yet turned thirty, Jack was starting to look older. "Remember how he used to tell us that his father would hit him with a belt if he broke eggs or bruised apples on the farm? How he taught himself to treat every egg and every apple like it was made of glass?"

Jack looked off into the distance. "I can't be like that. I don't want to treat every fishing pole and every hunting knife like it's the crown jewels. I hate his endless criticizing. If I were you, I'd go to London and never come back."

Willow squeezed his arm. "I don't fit in there. You can't really fit in anywhere else when you come from here. And Mummy tried her best to make us not fit in here either, didn't she?" She laughed.

"Everyone thinks I'm just like him, but I'm not," Jack continued, walking with her to Jeff's truck. "And he and Mum want me to be like him, but I can't do it."

"He needs you more than ever," Willow said, pulling the keys out of her pocket. "Without you, he couldn't take all these people out to the boonies and do the work it takes to make sure they have a good time. He's too old."

"I know. And those people pay the bills."

"I'm sorry, Jack. I didn't know you weren't happy. You're hard to figure out."

"That's what Tina used to say. She said she never knew what I was thinking. Keith is just the opposite. He spills his guts all over the place and never stops talking. Guess that's what she wanted."

"Oh, stop it," Willow said, climbing into the truck. "Now you sound like Dad. Come down to the cannery tomorrow and have supper with us. And try to get away from Dad when you aren't working. You stay at home too much." She put the key in the ignition.

"The problem is," Jack said, "I'm always working. The way he sees it, there's work and sleep, and nothing else. Anyway, tell Jeff I said hi. I'll try to come for supper."

"Good." She looked at him. "Why do you think I spent my childhood out in the woods drawing pictures and making up stories? It was the only way I could get away from them."

Jack closed the truck door. She rolled the window down and leaned out. "They've worked hard to do their best for us. They just aren't very happy. Mum is in the wrong place because of the war, and Dad can't be happy anywhere because of the war and the Depression and the way he was raised."

"He says thinking about being happy is for lazy people who don't have enough work to do. He says knowing you did your job right should make anyone happy."

"Then I should be really happy, cuz I'm a damn good slimer. And you're good at everything you do, Jack." She smiled at him and put the truck in gear.

Driving back to the cannery, she thought about how she'd feel without Jeff. Probably just as trapped and angry as Jack, except he, being the oldest and a boy, would always have gotten the worst of it from their father.

"I did it," Sammy crowed when he saw her walk past the open kitchen door on her way back to the slime house. She looked at him blankly. "I saved a dish of chicken pie for you. It's in your fridge. Gary tried to take the last helping for hisself, but I got to it first and said no, I was savin' it for Willow."

"What would I do without you, Sammy?" she said, laughing.

He wiped his hands on his apron and turned to go back in the kitchen, saying, "You don't need to butter me up. Go over there and get busy or Artie will be lookin' for you."

She pulled her knife out of the sheath on her belt to see if it needed sharpening.

CHAPTER 15

The ferry from Bainbridge Island rocked softly from side to side as it lumbered through the choppy water of Elliott Bay toward Seattle. Carole, sitting inside at a table, clutched her cup of black coffee and watched the city slowly getting nearer through the windows. The skyline had changed dramatically since she was a little girl growing up in Ballard, the only daughter of a Norwegian fisherman and his religious, tight-lipped Scottish wife. Her brothers were so much older than she was that she felt she had barely known them. Now they were all long gone—parents, brothers, husband—and here she was, at forty-eight, still trying to erase Ballard and Alaska from her memory and her life. Still trying to get into a mansion on Queen Anne Hill where, ever since she was a small child and had been taken on rainy afternoons to sit in a corner with her rag doll while her mother cleaned house for the wealthy owners, she felt she truly belonged.

When she was young, the granite and terra cotta Smith Tower building was the tallest in the city. The glowing blue light on top of it had seemed magical, a distant beacon at the center of all that was prosperous, elegant, and beautiful. For many years, she told herself that the Blue Fairy in her picture book lived in the tall, pointed tower and came out at night to sit on top of the building, casting her soft blue light for children everywhere to see.

Then, in 1962, long after she had married Tom Riversen and moved to Agate Cove, she had brought her children, Jeff, Susie, and Sherrie, down to Seattle to see the Space Needle, standing more than one hundred feet taller than the Smith Tower, and the Century 21 Exposition spread out around it.

They had visited the fair at night, and the twinkling lights, futuristic white arches, and graceful International Fountain had taken her breath away. The natural gas jet on top of the Space Needle, shooting a brightly colored flame up into the night sky above the flying saucer–shaped top of the structure, was a wonder to behold. *Yes*, she had thought, *the future will surely be like this*—bright, clean, and full of technological marvels like the Monorail and the Bubbleator, a large, transparent, bubble-shaped elevator designed to carry up to one hundred people at a time upward into the glorious World of Tomorrow.

Carole wanted to live in the House of Tomorrow, as long as it was on top of Queen Anne Hill. There, in that glowing vision of the twenty-first century, household dirt and drudgery would be of no consequence to housewives like her. She would have lots of time to zip around Seattle in her gyrocopter, while robots and machines did whatever needed to be done at home.

When it came time to fly back to Alaska, she had felt an empty, sinking feeling that she was leaving that dream of the future behind forever. Sherrie and Susie were sad to be leaving Frederick's and the Bon Marché and had stuffed their suitcases with as many new items of clothing as their now empty savings accounts would allow. They were giddy at the thought of starting the school year with clothes no other girl in their town could possibly own.

Only Jeff was eager to be going home. He missed his grandfather and hated the noise, smells, and crowds of people roaming around the city. When Carole asked him what he thought of the World of Tomorrow, he had laughed and said the future looked like it had too many gadgets and gizmos that would be broken and need paint all the time. He told her that if he had to live in Seattle, he would live on one of the houseboats on Lake Union because they reminded him of the cannery, except they were too close together.

As the ferry neared the dock, Carole pulled her thoughts away from the past and made one last dash to the ladies' room before they tied up. She had walked on board, so had a few more minutes to get ready to disembark than the passengers who were now madly scrambling down to the lower deck to get in their cars. She had been so lost in thought during most of the trip that she had barely given a thought to the day ahead. It wasn't going to be fun, but at least it wasn't raining. In fact, the weather was lovely, as often happened in Seattle in early September.

She felt confident and energetic in her new pink pantsuit with its flared legs and nicely tailored jacket. She had been careful to choose lipstick and nail polish that matched her outfit and, after a lot of practice, had become adept at getting around in high platform shoes, although she'd have to be careful not to let her mind wander. She didn't want to trip on the sidewalk while walking uphill from the ferry terminal to catch a bus to Frederick's.

A question she had been turning over in her mind ever since the ferry left Winslow was whether she should have brought her twin daughters with her. They would have made the day more pleasant for her, of course, but perhaps not for Donna. They always enjoyed having lunch and watching the Wednesday fashion show in the eighth-floor Tea Room, but in the end, she had left them at home. *Still*, she thought, *if they are going to be Donna's stepsisters and live in the same house with her, the sooner they all learned to get along, the better.*

Carole had already, in her mind, chosen and decorated their new bedrooms in Harry's red brick mansion. Her visits to his house had become more frequent over the past several weeks, to the point that she now felt quite at home wandering through the spacious, antiques-filled rooms, daydreaming about the changes she would make after she and her daughters moved in.

It was a musty old place, probably not given a good airing or cleaning since Harry's first wife, Audrey, had moved back to Boston in 1965. It needed sprucing up. Now that everyone was looking forward to the Bicentennial celebration in 1976, antiques and Colonial things were back in fashion, so some of it could stay, but really, how much of the genuinely old stuff could anyone live with without feeling like a hostage in a museum?

She was already sick and tired of the Early American things she had just installed in her own house. So dark and gloomy. So reminiscent of housework and life being lived too close to the bone. Of course, moving into the Lewis mansion, with its terraced gardens and glorious views, would be delightful, but she had already decided that the first thing she would do after marrying Harry would be to call the movers and ship everything Audrey had bought for the house straight back to Boston. Either that or donate it to charity. Then the painters could come in and do something about the drab wallpaper. She would make it clear to Harry that no second wife should be forced to live with her predecessor's things. As for the antique Chinese stuff that Harry had inherited from his great-uncle, it could be crammed into his study, where he could enjoy it without inflicting it on everyone else.

She looked in the mirror one last time and put her lipstick back in her purse. *The sixties were really so much more fun*, she thought. *The seventies are turning out to be an awful bore. Prices are constantly rising, the Boeing cutbacks have put so many people out of work, and the new trends in clothing and home decor are just plain ugly.*

Donna studied the menu in the Frederick's Tea Room, waiting for Carole to make an appearance. *The crab salad looks good*, she thought, *and then the "Maple Frango Frozen Dessert" after that.* She wondered if they still served it on chilled silver plates. It had been years, almost a decade, since she had been in there, not since her mother had moved out, and she had been sent away to boarding school in New England.

She might have known Carole would be late. What her father saw in that woman she would never know. *And who does she think she is, anyway? Her daughters' best friend, or their mother?* It was mortifying to think that Carole might become her stepmother.

"Well hello, dear!" Carole called out cheerfully as she followed the waitress across the elegant, thickly carpeted room, waving as she approached the table. "I had to wait forever for a bus."

All around the room, well-dressed older ladies, many of them wearing out-of-date hats with small veils, looked up from their fruit and cottage cheese plates, making Donna feel even more annoyed than she already was. She couldn't bring herself to admit that Carole looked stylish and svelte in her bright pink pantsuit.

Carole sat down on the spindly gilt chair that the waitress had pulled out for her. "That's a lovely coat, dear," she said, looking at the old camel hair coat Donna had thrown over the back of her chair. "Perfect for this time of year." She picked up her menu. "I've always thought it was so clever of them to sew the labels in upside down."

"I never noticed," Donna said, twisting around in her seat to look at her coat. "Why would they do that?"

"So people walking by the table could see where the coat was from, of course."

"How strange. Anyway, it was my mother's. She bought it in about 1960."

"Such good quality. Made to last." Carole smiled at the hovering waitress. "I'll have the fruit salad. With Melba toast." She turned to Donna. "What sounds good to you? Remember, it's my treat today."

Donna ordered the crab salad, then took a drink of water and looked at Carole. "I'm not really sure why you invited me to lunch," she said. "Dad needs me at the office, so I can only stay for an hour."

"Oh, I'm sure he won't mind if you stay away a little longer, not if he knows you're with me." Carole unfolded her linen napkin and spread it across her lap. "I thought we'd watch the fashion show and then do a bit of shopping."

"I don't need anything," Donna said, looking at her watch. "I have to be at a meeting in the office at one thirty. Sorry." She raised her hand and beckoned to a gray-haired waitress who was passing their table. "I'm in a hurry to get back to work. Could you ask the kitchen to get our order ready quickly?"

The waitress looked surprised, then nodded and scurried off in the direction of the kitchen. She had never had a request like that from one of her customers.

"We should have eaten at the counter downstairs in the Paul Bunyan Room," Donna said, sounding irritated. "It would have been faster."

"Do you mean that place in the basement where young men get sandwiches and milkshakes?" Carole asked, her eyes wide with amazement. "I buy their chicken pot pies to take home from time to time, but I've never thought of actually eating there. It's so loud and crowded. And the counter seating doesn't look comfortable. The stools look like they were made for Paul Bunyan himself."

"I like it down there," Donna replied. "The service is fast." *It's also a good place to meet men*, she thought, *but Carole doesn't need to know about that.* If Donna had learned one thing in boarding school, it was how to keep her mouth shut and be sneaky, especially where men were concerned.

Carole looked at Donna's ill-fitting plaid suit and said, "Surely, you must need some things for your trip to Alaska. It's only a few weeks away."

"I have what I need. We'll only be there three days."

"Three days! But that's not long enough to see or do anything."

The waitress arrived and placed their plates in front of them. She asked Donna, "Will you be wanting dessert, miss? I can put the order in now if you like."

"No, thank you. I was going to have something, but I really don't have time. We got a late start," she said, glancing at Carole.

Carole ignored the look. "I think you should stay in Alaska longer than three days," she said. "If I come with you, we certainly will. Your father and I have already discussed it."

Donna looked up from her crab salad. "Dad didn't say you were coming with us."

"He and I think I should, if we want this deal to go smoothly. Jeff is my son, after all. He's more likely to trust me than you." She smiled and calmly snapped a small piece of Melba toast in two.

"Dad has never brought a girlfriend with us on a business trip before," Donna said, narrowing her eyes. "I don't see why you need to be there. It won't take us long to look things over. We already have a pretty good idea what we're willing to pay."

"I don't see how you could," Carole said, spearing a grape with her fork. "Your father hasn't spoken to my son or seen the books yet. It's more complicated than you may realize, dear."

Donna looked at her salad, thinking, *If this awful woman calls me "dear" one more time, I will put my fork down and walk out of here.* Even her own mother never called her anything like that. No one in her family spoke that way. She tore off a piece of her roll and buttered it. "It may seem complicated to you, Carole, but it's not for us. I'm not even sure why my father thinks we should waste our time going up there. We could easily close this deal without a trip. Your son is either going to agree to our terms or he isn't."

"You do understand that you're talking about a business that has been in my husband's family for three generations, don't you? If you expect my son to come to terms, you're going to need my help. He doesn't like or trust outsiders."

Donna looked at her. "What's an outsider?"

"Anyone who hasn't lived in Alaska forever."

"That's ridiculous."

"You may think so, dear, but you aren't going to get what you want without my help." Carole sipped her ice tea. "And please stop referring to me as your father's girlfriend. It makes us sound like teenagers. We have a very serious, adult relationship."

"Dad's last girlfriend told me the same thing, and now I can't even remember her name," Donna said, standing up and brushing bread crumbs off her skirt. She yanked her coat off the back of her chair and picked her purse up off the floor. "I'm sorry. I have to go. Dad needs me at the office. We need to discuss taxes."

"Surely you have accountants for that," Carole said, reaching down to retrieve the napkin Donna had dropped on the carpet.

"We do, but I need to check their work. They miss things."

"My goodness, you are so terribly accomplished. Such a modern young woman. Well, run along, then. I'm having cocktails with your father this evening, and I'll be sure to tell him what a nice lunch we had."

Donna slung her brown leather purse over her shoulder and strode out of the Tea Room at a brisk pace.

Later that night, when Carole got home after drinks and dinner with Harry, she found Susie and Sherrie sprawled on the floor in front of the TV in their pajamas.

"Girls, it's late. Don't you have to work tomorrow?" she asked, closing and locking the front door. They had both found jobs in Winslow after their dance camp jobs had ended.

Susie looked up. "Mom, you look positively exhausted. Is old Harry wearing you out?" They both laughed.

"Oh, stop it. Don't say rude things, or I'll wash your mouths out with soap."

That made them laugh even harder. "Sorry, Mom," Sherrie said. "You know we think he's a pompous old phony."

"Everyone in your generation thinks everyone in my generation is an 'old phony,' whatever that means, just because we are polite and don't say crude things to each other. Harry is a successful man from a good background. You should want me to marry him." Carole sat down on the sofa and took off her shoes. Her feet were killing her. She began gently massaging the ball of her left foot. "What did you two do this afternoon?"

They looked at each other and smiled, then Susie spoke up. "We learned some interesting things about Donna."

Carole stopped rubbing her foot and looked at them. "What are you talking about? Do you mean Donna Lewis, Harry's daughter? You haven't even met her yet."

"No, but we heard a lot about her today." Sherrie giggled.

"How? Where?"

"After you left this morning, we decided to go horseback riding with one of the girls we met this summer. She was teaching equestrian skills to the campers and we got to be friends. Anyway, she boards her horse at a farm near Marysville where they have horses you can rent for trail rides."

"They're old, calm horses, not dangerous ones," Susie added.

"So," Sherrie went on, "we drove up there and while our friend—her name is Christy—was getting her horse, we asked her about the horse in the stall next to hers. She said it belonged to a rich, frumpy-looking girl named Donna who didn't ride it very much because whenever she came out to the farm she spent most of her time fooling around with the guys who work there. They have bedrooms behind the stables, and they all know her pretty well, if you get what I mean."

They began laughing. "We're not going to tell you what they call her," Susie added, catching her breath. "It's too rude."

"I don't believe it," Carole said, staring at them. "It must be someone else."

"No, it isn't, Mom. Christy said this Donna lives in a mansion on Queen Anne with her dad and thinks she's better than everyone else because she went to boarding school back East. She says the other girls don't like her because she never shuts up about her stupid old family in Boston, but the stable hands don't seem to mind."

"Girls, go to bed," Carole said, standing up and turning off the television. "I've got an awful headache. You are not to mention this to anyone. Do you understand? Good night!"

She picked up her shoes and walked slowly down the hall to her bedroom. Before closing the bedroom door, she stuck her head out into the hallway and shouted, "Now, girls! I said go to bed!" She heard muffled giggling coming from the living room, then closed the door firmly. What a hell of a day it had been.

CHAPTER 16

Jeff finished reading the last page of his mother's letter, then ab-sentmindedly smoothed it out with his hand. Her round, loopy handwriting, with lots of exclamation points and double-under-lined words, sprawled across both sides of three thin, blue sheets of airmail paper, getting smaller and smaller toward the end as she ran out of space on the last page. He had read the whole thing through twice and still wasn't sure what to make of it.

Outside his office window, the world was gray. Gray sky, gray buildings, gray ocean, gray gravel road. September rain pelted down, streaking the glass. He shivered and coughed.

The season was as good as over. The *Kitty Marie* was in today and the *Ashley B.* would be in tomorrow. Both would have such small loads of fish that it was hardly worth calling everyone in to can them. He had already sent a lot of people home for the winter. The ones who were still around could do just about any job in the place and would wrap things up for the year. The three slimers he had left could work on the canning line and then move into the warehouse to help John and Nancy. The rest of the warehouse crew was already gone.

It had been a good season. Lots of late nights and not too many days off. People had gone home smiling, knowing there was a lot of overtime pay in their bank accounts. Paul's sister had written to say he was doing better. He had stopped drinking and was working hard in their commercial pear orchard.

Kenny had turned out not to be one of Jeff's hiring mistakes. He and his wife were going to stay in town all winter. They both had jobs, and John had gotten him off whatever he was on. The baby was growing and beginning to talk.

Jeff didn't like thinking about the guys he had hired who hadn't made it. He had had to drive to the morgue too many times to identify their bodies and still dreamt about their pale, waxen faces when Willow was far away.

Those dreams would be back soon. Willow had bought her plane ticket to London and would be leaving before long. Jeff hated driving her to the airport and watching her walk away from him. She always turned around once or twice to wave goodbye with a lost look on her face.

Sometimes he felt like vomiting when he got back in his truck after she had gone. He would sit in the airport parking lot until he saw her plane take off and disappear into the clouds. He could never stop himself from waiting there for an extra half hour, just in case the plane turned around and came back, but it never did.

He folded the letter and stuffed it back in the envelope, then put it in one of the desk drawers and pushed his chair back. It was almost time for lunch. They'd be done by three today, at the latest. Should he wait until then to talk to Artie about what his mother had written, or go find him now, before lunch? He wanted to hear what he had to say before he discussed it with Willow, but he had to find a way to get him alone.

Artie was different from John. He could keep his mouth shut and was naturally suspicious and pessimistic, which usually turned out to be a good thing. He didn't think much of most people and thought they were nothing but trouble on the hoof, unlike John, who had a temper but tended to believe there was good in people even when there really wasn't.

After a few beers over at the Snowshoe, Nancy had once told Jeff that she'd seen John's wife's clothes and shoes in his bedroom closet, exactly where she'd left them five years ago. She had asked him why they were still there, and he'd said it was "for when she comes home from Michigan."

After hunting around for a while, Jeff tracked Artie down in the can shop. He had just finished unjamming a reformer for the third time that morning and looked fed up. Jeff knew at a glance that Darlene Simmons had been trying to flirt with him. She had probably jammed the machine on purpose, knowing it wouldn't make much difference to anyone if the line stopped on a slow day at the end of the season.

"Put those dangly earrings and that long necklace in your pocket now," Artie was saying to her, wiping grease off a wrench. "They're gonna get caught in this damn machine and kill you. How many times do you have to hear that?"

Darlene made a face. "Don't you like them? I like to look my best at work, unlike some of the girls around here."

"I don't want to see you wearing them again. Understand?"

"You wouldn't say that if we were dancing at the Snowshoe." She gave him a long look. "How come I never see you there anymore? Wife won't let you out of her sight? You used to be fun."

She reached behind her neck and pretended to fumble with the clasp on her necklace. "Help me undo this. I can't do it by myself."

Jeff walked over to her. "Here. I'll do it." He quickly undid the clasp and handed her the necklace. "You know the rules about wearing jewelry at work. If you don't want to follow them, you can punch out and go home."

Darlene stopped smiling and sat down on the stool next to the reformer. She grabbed a handful of flat can bodies from a box and shoved them into the loud machine.

"Artie, can I have a word?" Jeff shouted. "In private."

"Yeah, sure. Let's go out back."

They went outside and found a dry spot on the dock under the eaves. No one was around, the beach gang being occupied farther down the dock.

"That damn woman drives me nuts," Artie said, pulling a handkerchief out of his pocket and blowing his nose. "Why don't she stick to screwing around with Sylvester and leave the rest of us alone?" He looked at Jeff. "What's on your mind? We got another problem?"

"Not with anything going on right now." Jeff looked down the dock at the *Kitty Marie* bobbing up and down on the water. Dan was backing up the forklift. The sound of the backup alarm blew downwind along with the stinging rain. "I got a letter from my mother this morning. She says she's found a buyer for this place. Some rich guy in Seattle that she's been dating. He wants to buy her property out at the lake and everything I own down here—the buildings, the dock, the vacant land out back—all of it together. He says he won't buy her land if I don't sell. He wants one clean deal. She's all excited and wants to push this thing through right away. I don't think she's hard up, so she must be trying to get in good with him. She's been hunting for a rich husband ever since my dad died."

"Well, what do you want?" Artie said. "Seems to me you've about had it with running this place. Might be a good chance to get out."

"It might be, but something doesn't feel right. My dad told her not to sell that lake property unless she was desperate, which she isn't. I don't know a damn thing about this guy, but it's pretty clear he's got her under his spell."

Artie shoved his handkerchief back in his pocket. "No harm in meeting him, I guess. I'd tell her to stop dating him if I was you. Business and romance don't mix. Does she want you to go down to Seattle?"

"No. She says they're both coming up here in a few weeks to talk things over. And she says he's got a daughter who works for him and is some kind of business genius. She's coming too."

"What's the point of that? We'll be all shut down by then. Don't they want to see how the place works? Why come up here after the season's over?"

"I don't know. I can't figure it out." Jeff coughed and winced. His throat was starting to feel sore. "And I don't see why they have to get the lake property and this place all in one deal. It doesn't make any sense."

"Think they've really got any money?"

"I don't know that either. There's no way to find out until the lawyers get involved. Mom says he lives in a big house full of antiques from Boston and China, but that doesn't mean anything. Lots of people who are damn near broke have that kind of stuff lying around. Look at Willow's mother. She's got a ton of old crap from England, but she and Jim can't pay for Willow to go to school."

"Can't or won't? Jim Marsh wouldn't pay for anything that wasn't for fishing or hunting. Know anyone in Seattle who could do some snooping for you?"

"I might, but I'm gonna wait on that. Let's meet them first and see what they've got to say. You'll help me show them around, won't you? I expect they'll have a lot of questions about the equipment."

"Yeah, sure. When did you say they were coming?"

"In a few weeks," Jeff answered. "I'll let you know. And don't tell anyone. We're already losing people to Line jobs. We'll lose even more if they think new owners are taking over."

"You'll be losing me, too, if I don't like the looks of 'em. Keep that in mind. What about you? What are you gonna do if you sell up?"

"I have no idea. I never thought about it, to be honest. Maybe they'll want me to stay on and run things."

"You've been saying you wanted to get rid of this place ever since your grandpa died. You must have some idea what you want to do."

"I used to think I wanted a job where I wouldn't be stuck in one place all the time, but now I'm not so sure." Jeff zipped his jacket up and stuck his hands in his pockets. The rain was coming down in sheets now. He could barely see the end of the dock. "I think we Riversen men have some bad DNA in us that makes us restless."

"That's hogwash," Artie said, turning his back to the wind. "It ain't bad DNA. It's bad child-rearing. Your daddy couldn't settle down cuz he was dragged all over the place from one worthless mining claim to another by your grandpa when he was a youngster." He turned up the collar of his gray coverall and pulled his cap lower over his eyes. "He got a taste for roaming early on, just like some people get a taste for booze, and it ruined his life. Your grandpa felt real bad about that. That's why he bought this place. He used to say it was selfish and wrong of him to do that to your grandma and your dad, to make 'em keep moving around all the time. He tried to teach you to be different, to be happy staying put."

"I never saw much of my dad," Jeff said, looking at his watch as the piercing sound of the noon whistle suddenly cut through the wind and rain. "He was always away somewhere. He sent money home so we could have a nice house and all that, but to me and my sisters he was just a good-looking phantom who was never around. When he was home for a couple of days, he and Mom would fight.

She'd say he had something wrong with his head, and he'd say only stupid people were happy staying in one place all the time." He wiped his face with the back of his hand and coughed again.

"You never really knew him," Artie said, stomping his feet, "but I'm thinking you've learned enough since he died to know there wasn't anything too appealing about him."

"I know about the other women and the business partners he pissed off, if that's what you mean. Someone once told me he was a great liar because he didn't even know when he was lying." Jeff sneezed. "Damn. I think I'm getting a bug. Anyway, Mom said people laughed at him because he would tell their own stories back to them and not even know he was doing it. If he heard a good one from anybody, he'd take it for his own."

Artie smiled. "He did that to me more than once. And there was never any point in setting him straight cuz he'd just keep on doing it." He pulled his handkerchief out again and wiped his nose. "Jeez, it's nasty out here today. I can smell winter coming. You know, that last deal your dad got himself into wasn't very smart. Not sure how he would have gotten out of it if he hadn't gone down in that plane."

"Yeah, I know. Jim Marsh never stops telling me about it. He didn't like my dad one bit. Thought he was a flashy blowhard."

"And your dad thought Jim was a stubborn bastard who wouldn't take advice about anything from anyone. That's why Jim's always worked for himself. Thinks he's the only one who knows the right way to do anything. And he drives that son of his like a pack mule."

"Jim's a tough guy, but I can get along with him. It's Florence who doesn't like me. Let's go eat. Sammy said he was making chili for lunch."

As they turned to go back inside, Jeff added, "At least my mom and sisters are okay. She made sure Dad had a lot of life insurance and never let him touch the money she got from her parents. Then Grandpa left this place to me, so it all worked out."

Artie pulled the door open and they walked through the cannery in silence. Outside the bunkhouse, Jeff looked at him and said, "No one misses Dad. Maybe some of his old girlfriends do, but I doubt it."

"Hate to say it," Artie replied, "but I always thought he was just a slick charmer. He had a few tricks to make people like him, then used them and his handsome face to get what he wanted." He paused. "And if I know your mother, this new guy is gonna turn out to be just like him. She's naturally drawn to that type."

Willow sat down next to Jeff in the bunkhouse kitchen and began breaking crackers into her chili. "I don't like the sound of that cough," she said. "It's getting worse."

"It's nothing, Babe. Just a cold. I always get a cold in September. We all do." Jeff poured hot sauce into his chili and stirred it with a fork.

"After we finish work this afternoon, I'll go borrow Mother's steam inhaler. It works great with some Vicks." She began eating. "This chili is really good, Sammy. Did I see butterscotch pudding in the fridge?"

"I'm just about to get it out," Sammy answered. "Who needs coffee?"

Dan, eating with the beach gang at their table, looked up from his second bowl of chili and said, "I do. Damn, it's cold and wet out there today. Slippery too." Sammy poured a mug of coffee and set it in front of him. "Thanks, Sammy. Oh, by the way, Jeff, there's a leak in the roof upstairs, almost over Gary's bunk. We put a bucket under it, but the roof needs patching."

Jeff coughed. "We can try getting a tarp up there, but it'll probably blow off. Can't do a real patch in this weather."

"I wish you'd go to bed after lunch," Willow said. "You never get enough rest. Can I please have a little pudding now, Sammy?"

John, eating silently across from them, stood up to get more chili. "Better watch out, Jeff, or she'll have you tucked up in bed before you know it with your chest covered in Vicks and hot water bottles on your feet."

The beach gang started laughing. Jeff looked annoyed. "Shut up, John. I'm fine, Babe. Don't fuss."

Willow looked at him without saying anything, then went on eating her pudding. It wasn't like Jeff to be short-tempered like that, especially with John. They teased each other all the time about all sorts of things. He probably wasn't feeling well and didn't want to admit it.

"Sorry, John," Jeff apologized. "I feel crappy, and I've got a lot on my mind." He stood up and took his bowl to the sink. "I'll take a cup of coffee over to the office, Sammy. No pudding for me." Coming back to the table he leaned over and kissed Willow on the top of her head. "Sorry, Babe. Maybe that thing you're gonna get from your mom will help. Thanks."

At four o'clock, Willow opened the front door of her parents' house and walked in. "Mum?" she called out. "Where are you?" The house was silent. "Mummy?"

She walked into the empty kitchen and looked out the window into the backyard. Her mother's car was parked by the shed, but there was no sign of her in the vegetable garden or by the raspberry bushes. Willow didn't really expect to find her outdoors since it was still raining hard. She went back through the kitchen to the hall and walked down to her parents' bedroom. As she passed Jack's room, she heard a muffled sound from behind the closed door. Opening it, she found her mother sitting on the edge of Jack's bed, sniffling and wiping her eyes with a white, embroidered handkerchief.

"Mummy! What's wrong?"

"He's gone," Florence whispered. "Just this morning. We had no idea."

"Who? Jack? What are you talking about?" She sat down on the bed next to her mother.

"He never said a word about it before today to either your father or me. Just got in his truck early this morning and said he was driving to Valdez."

"Valdez? Why?"

"He said he'd been talking to friends all summer about how to get hired on at that Terminal Camp they're building down there, and he finally got a job offer, so he had to go."

"Really?" Willow looked around Jack's room. He had clearly packed in a hurry. Most of the dresser drawers were open or half-open. The closet door was wide open and empty hangers had been thrown in a pile on the floor. "Well, that's not really so bad, is it?" she said. "Those are good jobs. They pay a lot. Why are you so upset?"

"It's your father," Florence mumbled into her handkerchief. "Who's going to help him? He can't do all the work by himself, even if he thinks he can. He's so angry. I haven't seen him since Jack drove off at seven this morning. Dad got in his truck and left right after that."

"Where do you think he went?" Willow stood up and started tidying the room. She couldn't stand the mess Jack always lived with. Her own childhood room, just across the hall, was nearly empty, but she had kept it clean and neat all her life.

"He said he was going to the hardware store and Rod's Gun Shop, but that was hours ago. The stores weren't even open when he left."

"I'm sure he's mad, but he'll get over it. He'll be home for dinner." Willow picked a paperback book up off the floor and put it on a shelf over Jack's desk. "Give him a little time. Once he gets used to the idea, he'll be proud of Jack for earning all that money."

"Jack should never have left him in the lurch like that, with no warning at all." Florence wadded up the handkerchief and pushed it into her apron pocket.

"He probably didn't want Dad to argue with him and try to talk him out of it. You know how Dad gets when Jack tries to do things on his own."

"I know, but Dad says Jack doesn't do things the right way if he's left on his own. He worries about him all the time."

"Mum, Jack's almost thirty years old. He's a good guy. And he's never done anything Dad didn't approve of. This really isn't so bad."

Willow pushed the dresser drawers shut and closed the closet door. "I've heard they have people called bull cooks out there at the Terminal Camp who clean the rooms and make the beds. Jack's such a slob. He's going to think he's in a luxury hotel." She picked a blanket up off the floor and folded it. "And people say the food is great. He'll get fat."

Florence stood up and straightened her apron. "And what about your father? Who's going to help him while Jack's away getting maid service and eating rich meals?"

"Can't he hire someone? I bet he could find a helper somewhere in town."

"You know your father. It takes him a long time to get used to new people." Florence went out into the hall. "I need a cup of tea. Leave that mess and come with me. Why are you here at this time of day?"

"We finished early. There's not much work anymore." Willow followed her mother to the kitchen. "And I need to borrow your steam inhaler. You know, the one you used when we were kids and had colds? Jeff has a bad cough. Do you still have it?"

"I'm sure it's around here somewhere." Florence sighed. "We'll look for it after tea."

Chapter 17

Willow picked up a wooden spoon and stirred the bubbling pot of rhubarb chutney on her mother's stove. Her white cotton apron was already spattered with the raspberry jelly and lingonberry sauce she and Florence had made earlier that morning. The dark blue bandana covering her hair had flour on it from the bread dough she had made when she got to her parents' house at six thirty. She and Florence had been hard at work since then, trying to get so many things done before Jim came home with the moose.

"Mum, does this look right?" she asked. "If I cook it any longer, it's going to stick to the pot."

Florence stopped rolling and cutting doughnuts at the kitchen table, wiped her hands on a dish towel, and came over to the stove. "It's done," she said. "Ladle it into those clean jars over there." She glanced at the clock on the kitchen wall. "Look at the time! Almost one, and these doughnuts still have to rise a second time, and then there's the bread to bake. I hope your father doesn't get here too soon."

Willow moved the hot chutney off the stove and began carefully spooning it into jars. "I didn't get any breakfast this morning, Mum. I had to leave to get over here before Sammy or anybody else was up." She had suddenly become aware of her growling, empty stomach. "Is there anything in the fridge I can eat?"

"There's a bowl of leftover salmon salad," Florence said as she lined up doughnuts for their final rise.

"I can't look at salmon. Is there anything else?"

"Not much. With your father and Jack away, I haven't been cooking. There's some cheese."

Willow finished ladling the chutney and put a lid on each jar. "I'll process these after I eat," she said, putting the dirty pot in the sink and filling it with hot water.

The kitchen counters were already nearly covered in jars of clear raspberry jelly and burgundy lingonberry sauce. Florence had let the mashed raspberries sit out on the counter overnight, their juice slowly dripping through the fine cloth jelly bag into a bowl. She never let anyone squeeze the bag to make the juice come out faster, as that would make the jelly cloudy.

Willow pulled a block of bright orange cheese from the fridge. "Are there any crackers?"

"Look in the cupboard over the stove. You know where we keep them."

She sliced some cheese and ate it at the sink with the slightly stale crackers. She had been helping her parents get ready for winter for as long as she could remember. It was always a hectic time, with so much to do before the cold weather set in. Her father and Jack usually went duck hunting in the fall, but with Jack away for the first time, Jim hadn't felt up to going out on his own.

They could do without ducks, he had said, especially with only two people at home, but they couldn't do without moose, so he had gone down to the Snowshoe and asked Bob to go hunting with him. Willow knew how much he hated asking anyone outside the family for help, but this year he didn't have a choice.

Bob had four daughters and no sons and got along with Jim as well as anyone did, so he agreed to go. They decided they'd get Jim's moose first and then go out again a little later in the season to get a bigger one for Bob.

"When did you say your flight was?" Florence asked, filling the tea kettle with water.

"Saturday. I can't believe it's the last time I'll be making this trip. I'll be done before Christmas."

"I hope you'll change your mind and stay in London for a while. Give it some thought."

"I will, Mummy. Promise."

"You're so young. You should stay over there and enjoy yourself. Get a job. Make more friends. There's nothing here for young people, especially in the winter. You'll regret it when you're older if you give up this opportunity and come rushing back here."

"What about Jeff?"

"Plenty of fish in the sea. You haven't even had a proper look around yet."

Willow put the cheese back in the fridge and the crackers back in the cupboard. She didn't want to have this conversation again, didn't want to hear how her mother had ruined her life by leaving London and moving to miserable little Agate Cove, Alaska. She loved Jim, Florence would say, but no one would ever know how she much she had given up for him. Willow and Jack called it "The Martyr Speech."

At three, just as Willow was shaking the last of the warm doughnuts in a brown paper bag full of cinnamon sugar, she looked out the kitchen window and saw her father's truck coming into the yard. He pulled into the empty space next to the shed where Jack usually parked. She could see that the back of the truck was fully loaded with gear and big sections of the bull moose he had shot.

"Mum, Dad's back."

"Oh dear, sooner than I was expecting him," Florence said, turning the gas off under the deep kettle of hot fat where she had been frying doughnuts. "Here, hand me that bag. I'll finish them. They need to go in the freezer chest as soon as they cool off. Go out and help Dad."

Willow washed the sugar off her hands and went out the back door.

"Hi, Dad. How'd it go?"

"It was rough," Jim replied. "The damn thing was way back in the woods, standing in a pond. We had to pack the meat out in hip waders. I'm bushed." He started unloading the truck. His face looked gray, and his beard, which he hadn't shaved in a few days, was almost all white. For the first time, it crossed Willow's mind that her father was starting to look old.

"Did you see any bears?"

"No. We were lucky, considering how many trips we had to make to get it all out." Jim pointed at a white plastic bucket in the back of the truck. "The liver's in there. Take it in to Mother. She'll want to get it washed and cut up right away."

"She's going to want the tongue and heart too," Willow said, pulling the heavy bucket out of the truck. Looking down at the glossy, dark purple liver, she said, "It looks like a good one. What do you think it weighs?"

"Oh, probably about twelve pounds," Jim answered. "And tell her I gave the heart and tongue to Bob. He's got six mouths to feed, and we'll only have two with you and Jack gone. I'm going to give him some of this meat too, once it's butchered and wrapped up. We don't need all of it."

"Are you going to have Mr. Schneider make sausages out of some it? We all like them, especially in Mum's sausage rolls at Christmas."

"Yeah. The old man's not working much anymore. He goes back to Germany every fall to see what's left of his family, so his son has taken over. He's a good boy."

Willow heard the note of bitterness in her father's voice. He was still angry with Jack for letting him down. She said quickly, "I've always wondered, was Mr. Schneider on the other side in the war?"

"No. No, he wasn't. His parents moved to Seattle when he was a boy, just before the first war, and then he moved to Alaska after he worked for the Allies during the second one." He handed her a duffel bag full of dirty clothes. "Take this inside." Frowning, he looked at her and said, "You don't think I'd do business with any German who was on the other side, do you?"

"I don't know. It was a long time ago."

"Not for me it isn't."

Willow carried the duffel bag and the bucket into the kitchen. "Mum, here's the liver," she said, setting the bucket down on the kitchen floor. "I'm taking these dirty clothes to the laundry room. I'll start a load."

"Don't forget to rinse the blood out with cold water first."

"I won't." Her mother always said that, as if she didn't know that Willow had been doing laundry and rinsing out blood stains all her life.

Florence looked in the bucket. "That's a nice big one. Where are the heart and tongue?"

"Dad gave them to Bob because we don't really need them and he has six people to feed."

Florence looked disappointed. "Oh. Well, he's right of course, but he does love the heart baked with bread stuffing. It was kind of him to give it to Bob. I was thinking you and Jeff could come over on Friday and we'd have it for dinner before you leave town." She lifted the liver out of the bucket with both hands and lowered it into the sink. "Bob's wife will be glad to have it."

"Jeff and I are doing something by ourselves Friday night. Can we come over on Thursday?"

Florence turned the cold water on. "If you'd rather. I assume he's taking you to the airport."

"Yeah, Mum. He always does."

Jim came into the kitchen through the back door. "Hello, Mother. I'm back. Did you clean the work tables in the shed?"

"Hello, dear," Florence answered. "Yes, Willow did that first thing this morning."

"Good." He looked at Willow. "Let's get the hide off that thing."

"I'll be right out. I have to start a load of laundry."

A few minutes later, she took a doughnut from the kitchen counter and went outside, munching as she walked to the truck. Jim was already there, waiting for her. "Here," he said, "get a grip on this. Once we get it on the table, skin it down to the knuckle."

"Okay." She grabbed the lower part of the leg while Jim picked up the upper part of the heavy hindquarter. Together, they carried it into the shed and set it on one of the two black and white, enameled work tables. Willow picked up a sharp knife and began working the skin off, starting at the top.

She looked out the open shed door at her father as he lifted the next section and began to carry it in by himself, staggering under the weight. Setting her knife down, she rushed to help him.

"Your brother should be here to help," he said breathlessly as she got hold of the other end.

"It's okay, Dad. I've got it."

"He knows how much I need his help this time of year. Why the hell couldn't he wait till winter to run off like that?"

"He didn't just run off. Maybe they told him the job wouldn't be there if he waited. He didn't do it to make things hard for you."

Jim found another knife and began working silently. After a few minutes he said, "I always thought Jack would take over the business when I got too old for it. Now it looks like he doesn't give a damn about everything I've taught him and done for him."

"That's not fair," Willow said, looking up. "This job he got in Valdez won't last forever. He'll come back and have some money in the bank too. You'll be proud of him."

Jim didn't say anything, so she went back to work, pulling the hide with her left hand and cutting it away with her right. They worked in silence, side by side, lost in their own thoughts, until Florence called them in to supper at six o'clock.

"What are we having, Mother?" Jim asked as he washed his hands and face at the kitchen sink.

"Liver and onions. And fresh bread we made this morning."

"Is there any cranberry ketchup, Mum?" Willow asked.

"We've still got a little from last year. I don't think I'll make a new batch if you aren't here to help. Go look in the pantry."

"Are you making raspberry cordial for Christmas?" Willow asked as she sat down at the table and opened the jar.

"I don't know. Maybe. It won't be much of a Christmas with Jack in Valdez and you in London." Florence began slicing bread on a pig-shaped cutting board that Jack had made in seventh grade wood shop.

"I won't be in London, Mummy. And Jack will probably get some time off and come home too."

"But I want you to stay in London. What on earth are you going to do with your education and talent in a place like this? Tell her to stay over there, Jim, at least until next summer." Florence passed a dish of cooked cabbage. Willow took a spoonful and looked at her father.

"Jack sure as hell better get more than a few days off," Jim said, buttering a slice of bread. "I've got lots of things for him to do when he gets home."

Willow thought, not for the first time, that it didn't matter to her father if she stayed in London or not. What he cared about was having Jack around to help him.

"There's no place like London during the holidays," Florence went on, following her own train of thought. "The music, the lights, the mince pies."

Willow took a small bite of liver, drowning it first in cranberry ketchup. She didn't like it, but knew how hard her father worked to put food on the table, so she ate it.

"Do you need help after dinner?" she asked him.

Jim looked up from his plate. "I think we'll call it quits for today. I'm beat."

"Willow leaves on Saturday," Florence said. "She and Jeff are coming to dinner on Thursday."

Jim grunted. "Maybe Jeff can help me with a few things. Get here early tomorrow," he said, looking at Willow. "There's a lot more to do. Jeff won't need you, will he? He must be about ready to shut things down and close the place up."

"I'll come as early as I can. There's a boat coming in, but it won't be full."

"Mother will need more help too."

Florence stood up and started clearing the table. "Help me put those jelly jars away before you go," she said. "I need the counters clear if we're going to grind meat tomorrow."

Later that night, when Willow was soaking in the old green bathtub, Jeff came into the bathroom to take a shower. "You were gone a long time," he said. "What were you doing?"

"Oh, you know, the usual. Baking bread and doughnuts. Making raspberry jelly, lingonberry sauce, and rhubarb chutney. Skinning moose."

"Your clothes were a mess, especially that apron," he laughed. "I put it in the sink to soak."

"Thanks. I was too tired to do anything except get in the tub."

He walked over and kissed her damp forehead. "How's your dad managing without Jack?"

"He's having a hard time. He got Bob to go hunting with him. You know, today was the first time I ever looked at him and thought he was getting old."

"He is getting old. He must be, what, fifty-five, sixty?"

"He'll be fifty-eight in January."

"He's still in pretty good shape."

"I guess so, but when he got back with the moose today, I saw he hadn't shaved for a few days and his beard was all white. And he was struggling to get the hindquarters out of the truck."

Jeff yawned. "I'm not feeling so young myself right now."

She looked at him. "Did you have a bad day?"

"Not really. Just trying to get everything finished up. Sy and Lavinia left this afternoon. They stopped by to pick up her last paycheck on their way out of town."

"I wonder if they'll be back next year. They're getting old too."

"I hope not. They cause too much trouble."

"Hand me a towel, please. Dad wants me over there again tomorrow. They can't possibly get all this work done by themselves."

Jeff helped her out of the tub.

"Mummy was going on again about me staying in London, but how will they get by without Jack and me here? They already aren't doing a lot of things they used to do. The place is getting run down, and Dad didn't go duck hunting. The garden was a mess this year. I don't think Mum cares about it anymore."

"I'll come over tomorrow and help," Jeff said, putting his arms around her. "You don't want to stay in London, do you?"

Chapter 18

Carole tottered down her driveway in high-heeled gold sandals, hitching up the long skirt of her aqua chiffon gown with both hands. It was almost dark, and there were no streetlights nearby. She wished she had brought a flashlight, but it wouldn't have fit in her tiny, gold mesh evening bag.

At the bottom of the drive, she looked both ways, then scurried across the road. Once safely on the other side, she turned left and walked along the shoulder, crunching through debris that had fallen from the tall trees lining the road, until she came to an imposing cedar gate. She had driven past it many times, hoping to catch a glimpse of the house, but had never seen it open until this evening.

Two handsome young men in tuxedos were talking to each other just inside the gate. The two-way radios in their pockets hissed and crackled. Raucous '60s dance music blasted from a sprawling cedar and glass house on the far side of a lush, manicured lawn. When she came into view, one of the men stepped forward and took her arm.

"Let me help you, miss," he said, guiding her through the gate and over to a paved, well-lit path that led down a gentle slope to the front door. "Would you like me to escort you to the house?"

Carole let go of her skirt and smoothed her hair. "No, thank you. I can manage."

"The door is open, ma'am. Go right in and join the party," the other one said, looking her up and down in a way that made her feel like a seductive young woman again instead of a middle-aged matron about to stumble and fall on her face in the dark.

She smiled, put her shoulders back, and started down the path to the house.

The view of the Seattle skyline through the soaring wall of glass in the main room stopped Carole in her tracks. The Space Needle, skyscrapers, harbor, and ferries sparkled like distant, twinkling Christmas lights. The house seemed to float above the dark water of Puget Sound like a sleek private yacht, forever headed toward, but never quite reaching, the city.

Dozens of party guests who appeared to be about her age were crammed together in the vast, shag-carpeted room, drinking highballs and martinis and sending roars of laughter and clouds of cigarette smoke up to the vaulted, beamed ceiling thirty feet above her head. Barefoot women in satin gowns and tuxedoed men with open collars were doing the twist and the frug on an open, railed gallery that ran the length of the room on the second floor. Cherry red built-in sofas lined a conversation pit in front of an enormous sandstone fireplace at the far end of the room. Music pounded out of hidden speakers in the walls.

Carole bent down to remove her sandals. The thick, white shag felt delightful between her toes. Holding her shoes and evening bag in one hand, she went off in search of her host and a drink.

The waiter, Keith's brother, stood at the side of the table in the dark restaurant, pencil in hand. Tall and thin, his long face was scarred from teen acne. He had tried every cream and ointment in the drugstore, but nothing had worked.

"You look exhausted, Steve," Willow said, looking up from her brown, faux-leather menu.

"I've been helping Keith with the taxi at night," he yawned.

"I'm sure he appreciates it," Jeff said, closing his menu.

"Are you still living at home?" Willow asked.

"Yeah. Dad likes having me around now that Mom's gone."

"I just heard about that. I'm so sorry."

"Thanks. We never thought she would go first."

Looking across the table at Willow, Jeff asked, "Have you decided?"

"I'll have the fried chicken and a Shirley Temple."

"Fried shrimp and a beer for me."

Steve tucked the menus under his arm and turned to go, saying, "We aren't busy. It shouldn't take long."

The Beluga Room, on the ground floor of the Agate Inn, was the nicest restaurant in town. Catering mainly to summer visitors, it was deserted this late in the season. Willow and Jeff always went there before she had to go back to London.

"I love that dress. Thanks for wearing it," Jeff said, reaching across the table for her hand. "I'm going to miss you so much."

Tears welled up in her eyes and she bit her lip. "Is that the new sweater your mom sent? The color is great on you."

She squeezed his hand, then pulled hers away when Steve came back with the drinks. He set her Shirley Temple on the table. "The bartender wants to know why there's a kid in here at this time of night."

"You know me, Steve," she laughed. "Booze makes me feel like I need to go to the hospital."

"I know. He's an outsider. Doesn't know anyone yet." He put Jeff's beer down in front of him. "I'll go see how things are coming along in the kitchen."

Jeff took a swallow and looked at her. She had pinned her hair up, but some of it was already falling down around her face. In the shadowy darkness, surrounded by crushed gold velvet upholstery and midnight blue flocked wallpaper, she looked like a moon goddess, about to be carried away from him by the cold night wind. "We should leave for the airport at eight. Are you done packing?"

"Yeah. I finished this afternoon."

"How long do you have to wait in Anchorage for the flight to London?"

"About four hours. I've got my sketch pad and a book. And a candy bar."

"Write to me as soon as you get there, okay? Or send a postcard."

"I will." She stirred her Shirley Temple with the plastic swizzle stick, mixing the red syrup into the Seven-Up and pushing the maraschino cherry down to the bottom of the glass. "What are you doing tomorrow? I mean after you drop me off?"

"We have to get ready for those people from Seattle. Dan and Nancy are coming in to help. And John and Artie, of course. We're gonna do a lot of pressure washing and painting."

"Is your mother coming up?"

"Last time I heard from her, she said she was." He took another drink of beer. "I can't figure it out. She's trying to push this deal through, but she says she doesn't need money. And she says she doesn't know why this guy won't buy her property if I don't sell mine. It doesn't make sense."

"All right, here you go. The plates are hot." Steve set his loaded tray on a folding stand next to the table. He served them, picked up the tray, folded the stand, and carried both away, saying, "Holler if you need anything."

Willow started unwrapping foil from her baked potato. "I know one thing. This guy is going to be slick. Remember how she used to be in love with all the TV game show hosts? Sherrie and Susie and I teased her about it. Your mom would sit on the edge of the couch and stare at those guys in a trance."

Jeff dipped a shrimp into a cup of tartar sauce. "I imagine that's why she fell for my dad. He could manipulate just about anyone if he wanted to. You should have seen his closet. He had more suits than Johnny Carson. When he ran out of space, he filled up all the other closets. They used to fight about it because she was a clothes horse too." He spooned sour cream onto his potato. "Do you remember him?"

"Not really. He wasn't around much when I was playing with your sisters, and he never went to school events. Your mom always came alone. He honked at me once when I was on crossing guard duty in sixth grade. I think he wanted me to get the little kids across the street faster. They kept slipping on the ice and falling down in their snowsuits."

"That sounds like him. He was always in a big rush, acting like what he was doing was more important than anything anyone else was doing."

After Steve had cleared their plates, he asked, "Do you want dessert? There's banana cream pie. And there might be some chocolate cake, but I'd have to check on that."

"You want dessert, Babe?"

"No, thanks. I'm full. That was good."

"How much is it?" Jeff asked, looking at Steve. He took his wallet out and handed him a few bills.

"Why'd you wear a thin rain jacket on a night like this?" Jeff asked, holding Willow's coat.

"Everything else is either packed or too shabby to wear with a dress." She called across the deserted dining room, "Goodnight, Steve. I hope you get some rest."

"Not likely, this being Friday," he answered. "It's dead in here, but the Snowshoe is hopping. I'll be busy as hell after midnight, driving all those drunks home."

"Maybe you can take a nap now."

"Maybe. Hey, it's good to see you guys. How's Jack doing in Valdez?"

"We haven't heard much, but it sounds like he's okay. He isn't a letter writer and it costs too much to call."

"I'm trying to get a job out there myself. That kind of pay won't be around forever."

"That's what I tell my dad when he complains about Jack. You'd think he'd understand, but he doesn't."

Drink in hand, Carole worked her way through the crowd toward a man who had been pointed out to her as the host and homeowner, Bill Scott. She had found an invitation to the party in her mailbox one morning, but had never met him.

"Bill!" she called from a few feet away, waving her glass in the air. "It's Carole! Your neighbor from across the street and a few houses down."

Bill turned away from a man he had been conversing with and smiled in her direction. "Let's talk about it later," he said to the man, then waved at Carole. "Can you get through?"

She dodged around a couple who were locked in each other's arms, swaying unsteadily as if they might topple over at any moment, and popped up almost under Bill's nose. She tried not to spill her drink down the front of his impeccably tailored white dinner jacket. "Oh, my goodness. What a party!"

"We meet at last," he said. "I've heard about you. How did you find me in this mob?"

"Someone said to look for the good-looking guy in the white jacket."

"Ha! I guess it does make me easy to spot."

"You don't see white jackets around here much. Even at the opera."

"I wouldn't know. You'll never catch me at anything that stuffy."

Carole looked at him more closely and decided he was indeed good-looking, in a sexy, Tom Jones sort of way, with long sideburns and thick, curly brown hair.

"Is your wife here?" she asked, gazing up at him with wide blue eyes. "I should thank her for the invitation."

"I'm afraid not. There's no wife, no children, nobody but me. I've been a rolling stone until now and haven't collected any moss. That's why we've never met. The house has been closed up almost since the day I bought it."

Carole felt something like a heavy stone sinking down to the bottom of her stomach. She frowned, wondering if she had just met another restless, itinerant charmer like her late husband. They seemed to be everywhere. Perhaps it was time to go home and call Harry. He'd still be awake.

"That's all going to change now," Bill said, looking admiringly at her plunging neckline and slim waist. "My work has kept me wandering around Florida and the Caribbean, which accounts for the white dinner jacket, but I'll be staying here from now on."

"Is that right? What kind of work do you do?"

"Oh, you'd think it was boring. Something to do with boats."

She took a step back, feeling certain that it was time to leave. Boats could only mean one thing. Fish. "I'm feeling a little faint," she said, handing Bill her drink. "I should go home."

He set the glass on a nearby table and put an arm around her shoulders. "Please don't. You just got here. Let's go out on the deck and get some fresh air."

As he led her outside, she asked, "When you said boats, did you mean fishing?"

He looked down at her and laughed. "No. What made you think that?"

"Everyone I've ever known who worked around boats was in the fish business." They leaned against the deck railing and looked at the city across the water. "I grew up over there, in Ballard," she said. "My father was a fisherman. Then I lived in a small town in Alaska where my father-in-law had a fish cannery and everyone talked about fishing all the time."

"Which town was that?"

"It doesn't matter. They're all the same."

"No, really, where was it? I've been looking at maps of Alaska lately."

"It was an awful little place called Agate Cove. I called it Agony Cove."

Outside, a freezing wind blew pieces of trash down the street from one closed storefront to another. Jeff put his arm tightly around Willow's shoulders and she put her arm around his waist. They walked in silence to the parking lot and climbed into the truck. On the way back to the cannery, they listened to the only radio station in town.

After George Harrison's song "Give Me Love" finished playing, Jeff clicked on the high beams and said, "That's you, Babe. You give me all those things. Just like the song."

She moved closer to him on the bench seat. After a few minutes, she whispered, "I don't want to get on the plane tomorrow."

"I know, but you've got to. You've got to finish things up over there."

"I'm going to get my final project done as fast as I can. I'm not going to waste any time."

"You never waste time. You don't know how."

"Just like you."

"It's a good way to be."

Walking by the bunkhouse, they saw a light on in the kitchen. Inside, Sammy was kneading a soft, white mound of dough on a wooden cutting board. They stopped and went inside.

"What are you making at this hour?" Jeff asked, getting a drink at the sink.

"Cinnamon rolls. They gotta be ready by six," he said, looking at Willow, "so you can have some before you leave."

Willow walked over and kissed him on the cheek. "Thanks, Sammy. I'm going to miss you."

"You can't go flyin' with nothing in your stomach. Hand me that bowl of brown sugar and cinnamon. It's over there."

Jeff handed it to him. "Come on. Let's get out of here. If the rolls are ruined, he'll say it was our fault."

It was even colder and windier at the cannery than it had been in town. Willow shivered in her thin dress and jacket.

"Let's get inside before you freeze," Jeff said, unlocking the apartment door and holding it open for her. In the living room, her scuffed, blue suitcases waited, ready to be loaded into the truck the next morning.

She headed for the bedroom, tossing her raincoat on a chair and pulling out hairpins. As her hair cascaded down her back, Jeff, watching from the doorway, felt the sting of tears in his eyes. He turned and locked the door.

Chapter 19

The sun was beginning to rise behind Mount Rainier, bathing its upper slopes in warm, pink light, when Carole, strapping her sandals back on, said goodnight to Bill.

"Are you sure you don't want me to walk you home?" he asked, surveying the room and rubbing the stubble on his chin. Several guests were snoring gently on the sofas in the conversation pit. His housecleaners worked around them, emptying ashtrays and picking up glasses. "I could use some fresh air."

"No, you stay here. I'll be fine." She straightened up and smiled at him. "I can't remember the last time I had so much fun."

"Why don't you come back later and have lunch with me?"

"That would be lovely, but I can't. I have a lot to do today. I'm going up to Agate Cove next week."

"Really? I thought you hated the place."

"I do, but I have to get my son, Jeff, out of there before it's too late. He's been running my father-in-law's nasty old salmon cannery and is too involved with a girl who works there. If I don't do something, he'll be stuck in that hole for the rest of his life."

"What can you do?"

"Well, I happened to meet some really clever people recently who are interested in buying him out as long as I sell them some worthless land my husband left me at the same time." Looking down at her skirt, she sighed, noticing a stain running down the front. Someone had splashed rum and Coke on her, and she hadn't been able to blot it all out in the powder room.

"Why do they want it?"

"I have no idea, and, quite frankly, I don't care. They told me they invest in property all over the place and hold it for a long time."

Bill walked her to the front door. "When are you going?"

"Wednesday. They want to get this done and be back in Seattle by Friday. I'd like my son to move down here before Thanksgiving."

"Do you mind telling me who they are?"

"Oh, there's no reason you would have heard of them. It's a father-and-daughter business. Harry and Donna Lewis. I'm counting on them to help me."

Carole opened her eyes a little after noon, sat up in bed, and reached for the phone on her nightstand. A few moments later, Jeff answered.

"Cove Packers."

"Hi, honey. It's me."

"Hi, Mom. What's up?"

"I wanted to make sure you'll be ready for us on Thursday morning. We're getting there Wednesday, but we'll just go straight to the hotel."

"I told you we'd be ready."

"I know, but I'm worried."

"Do you want me to pick you up at the airport?"

"No, we'll get a taxi. We can't all fit in your truck, and it probably smells like fish."

"Whatever you want."

"Now listen, honey. These friends of mine aren't used to being around people like Sammy. I think it would be best if you kept him out of sight when we're there. He might say something that would spoil the deal."

There was a moment of silence, then Jeff said, "This call is costing you a lot. We'll talk when you get here."

"Can you at least make sure everyone is wearing clean clothes?"

"I've got to run, Mom. Bye." The line went dead.

She put the phone down, rearranged the pillows behind her back, then picked it up again.

"Hello?"

"Florence? It's Carole Riversen. How are you?"

"Carole? What a surprise! Are you calling all the way from Seattle?"

"Yes, I am. You see, there just wasn't time to write. I'm going to be in Agate Cove for a couple of days next week, and I was hoping to see you on Wednesday. Could we meet for coffee? I'll be staying at the Inn."

"Why yes, I don't see why not. Is there something particular you want to discuss?"

"I'm sure you can guess. We need to have a little chat about the children. I expect you're just as worried about them as I am. About how, shall we say, seriously entangled they've become."

"Much too entangled," Florence agreed. "They're so young and haven't done anything to broaden their horizons or meet other people."

"That's it, exactly. They have their whole lives ahead of them. Wouldn't it be a shame if they never moved out of Agave Cove or dated anyone else?"

"I've been trying to explain that to my daughter, but she won't listen."

"I think it's time you and I sat down and put our heads together, don't you?"

"I most certainly do."

"I knew you would. I've got to run now, but I'll call you when I get there."

"I'll be waiting. I'm sure we can come up with something."

"I know we can. After all, we both want what's best for them."

"Of course, we do."

"I'm so glad that's settled. See you soon!" Carole put the phone down, relaxed back into the pillows, and smiled. Florence was a dreary old thing, but not stupid. They'd find a way to pry those kids out of that disgraceful little nest of theirs at the cannery, introduce them to new people, and make them see what they'd been missing.

Steve felt his eyes closing and his mind drifting as he waited in the taxi outside the airport, listening to local news on the radio. It was almost three, and the people he was supposed to pick up at two hadn't arrived. The plane from Anchorage was usually late, sometimes by an hour, sometimes by a day or two, depending on the weather.

He pulled off his black watch cap, folded it in half, wedged it between his face and the window, and fell asleep. The next thing he knew, someone was rapping loudly on the passenger window. He woke with a start, not quite remembering where he was or what he was doing. Reaching over, he rolled the window down. An angry young woman in a long camel hair coat glared at him.

"Did someone send you to pick up a party of three from Anchorage?" she snapped.

"Uh, yeah." He turned the radio off, put his cap back on, and got out of the taxi. A blond, middle-aged woman and a gray-haired older man were standing next to a pile of luggage a few feet away. The man was also wearing a camel hair coat.

"Is that you, Steve?" the blond woman called out to him. "Where's Keith?"

He blinked and stared at her with his mouth half open. "Is that you, Mrs. Riversen? I didn't recognize you at first."

"Well, it's been a while. You were about thirteen when we moved away. You remember Susie and Sherrie, don't you? They're very accomplished young ladies now."

"That's good. We used to chase each other around the ice rink at school. What brings you back?"

"I'm here with my friends to do a little business."

The man smiled and stuck his hand out. "Harry Lewis. And this is my daughter, Donna."

The young woman scowled. "Can we get a move on? I could use a shower and a stiff drink after that hideous flight."

Mrs. Riversen hadn't really changed very much, Steve decided, but her friends weren't like anyone he'd ever seen, and he'd been working at the Inn and studying outsiders since he was fourteen. The daughter looked to be in her twenties but already had a furrow between her eyes and faint lines running from her nose to her downturned mouth. When she spoke, her jaw barely moved.

Her father's suntanned face and perfectly trimmed, silver hair made him look like a movie star. He wore dark, aviator-style sunglasses, apparently unaware that the sky was completely overcast and black storm clouds loomed above the mountains. *Who are these people?* Steve wondered as he stowed their monogrammed leather suitcases in the trunk. *And what is Jeff's mother doing with them?*

Donna climbed into the back seat, clutching her alligator handbag to her stomach as if she thought Steve might tear it away from her and disappear into the alder thicket across the road.

Harry helped Carole in beside her, then got in front next to Steve. "Agate Inn, young man," he said. "That's right, isn't it, Carole?"

"Yes, that's right."

"Is there any place better, driver?" Donna asked.

"No. It's the nicest place in town."

They splashed through a row of potholes. A spray of rain hit the windshield and Steve turned the wipers on. One of them—the wiper on the passenger side—wasn't working. "You won't be disappointed," he said. "The Inn has a nice bar and a good restaurant."

"It sounds just fine," Harry said. "And it's only for two nights. We'll be home before you know it, honey."

"I still think we could have done this deal without wasting so much time coming here, Dad."

Steve was already working out in his mind what he'd tell everyone at the Snowshoe later that night. They'd like hearing about Harry's suntan and Donna's gold earrings that looked like miniature lion head doorknockers. *What kind of deal is she talking about?* he wondered.

He knew more about what was going on around town than most people, since he worked at the Inn, drove the taxi, and dated a girl who worked at the radio station, but he hadn't heard anything about outsiders coming up to do deals.

After a few minutes, Harry asked, "Have you lived here all your life, Steve?"

"Born and raised."

"What's it like? Can young people like you find jobs? Or do they have to leave town for work?"

"Most of us get by, one way or another. Something always seems to turn up. The winters are kinda slow, but there's plenty to do in the summer, what with construction and fishing and tourists. And there's always the cannery if nothing better comes along. Sorry, Mrs. Riversen. I don't mean to say anything bad about it."

Donna seemed interested. She leaned forward a little. "Have you worked there?"

"Oh, yeah. Sure. It's hard, but if you get enough overtime you can come out okay. Depends on how the fish are running. This year was pretty good." He turned onto the main road. "I don't need to work there now, but I know people who do. Some of them have been there for years."

Harry, who had been looking at the scenery out the window, said casually, "Carole, you mentioned your father-in-law bought it a long time ago."

"He did, but he never had a head for business. My son has done a marvelous job turning it around. You'll be impressed when you meet him and see what he's done."

"I'm surprised he hasn't sold up and moved to Seattle to be with you and his sisters."

"He was close to his grandfather and let the old fool fill his head with romantic nonsense about life on the last frontier."

"If I was in his shoes," Steve butted in, "I'd never sell or leave town. I mean, he's not even thirty, and he's already got a perfect life."

They pulled up in front of the Inn, and he jumped out to get the suitcases. "Reception's in there, on the right," he said, pointing to a set of glass doors. "I'll bring the bags in."

Florence sipped her tea and grimaced. She added more milk. No one in Alaska knew how to make a proper cup of tea. She didn't know why she had ordered it. The lemon cake, which Carole had suggested, was quite good, though she noticed Carole hadn't touched hers. *Trying to stay slim*, Florence thought, *so she can borrow her daughters' clothes.*

Carole took a swallow of black coffee. "Now," she began, "I'm sure you've got some bright ideas about how to fix our little problem. It seems to me we could start by finding a way to keep Willow in England. If we could do that, then I think I could persuade Jeff to move to Seattle. He'll be much happier there, in the long run, than he ever would be here."

"I've told Willow she owes it to herself to stay in London, but she's childish and thinks she and Jeff can't live without each other."

"Nonsense. Neither one of them knows the first thing about life or love."

"I blame myself for reading her too many fairytales when she was young."

"Is there any chance she might take an interest in someone over there?"

"I have a thought about that." Florence ate a bite of cake. She had no intention of wasting a morsel of it, even though Carole was paying. "There's a young man teaching at the high school who wants to move to London and become a writer. His mother is an old school friend of mine. I think he and Willow are very well suited. If I could get her to spend some time with him over there, I think she'd see that I'm right."

"Excellent! But when will he get there? If he stays here until summer, it won't work."

"True, but things aren't going well for him at the high school. You know what kind of students the teachers have to put up with, not to mention the parents. He told me in confidence that he's not coming back after Thanksgiving. I encouraged him to go to London in early December."

"That's a couple of months from now, but we'll have to make it work. Would it help if you told Willow that Jeff seems to be taking an interest in someone else? I'm here on business with a friend from Seattle and his daughter. She's about Jeff's age, not attractive, and not the right one for him, but Willow doesn't need to know that. We're visiting the cannery tomorrow, so he'll be meeting her."

"Perhaps I could write and say Jeff is interested in this young lady."

"And I could tell him that this teacher you mentioned is going to London to see her. He doesn't need to know that—what's his name?"

"Alex."

"That Alex is going there for his own reasons. I could say Willow asked him to come over. Would that be going too far?"

Florence finished her tea, even though it tasted awful, and set her cup down. "We must do what we feel is best for the children and not worry too much about stretching the truth. It's for their own good, after all."

"I couldn't agree more." Carole looked at her untouched piece of cake. "Would you like to take this home? I'm having dinner in the Beluga Room later and can't fill up now."

"If you're sure. It would be a shame to throw away good cake."

"I'll be here until Friday morning. Call me if you have more ideas. Room 204. And thank you. I know we haven't always seen eye-to-eye, especially when the girls were young, but I'm glad we're in agreement now."

"We are indeed. And do ring me if you have new thoughts."

"I will. Yes, of course I will."

Chapter 20

Donna knocked on Harry's door. "Are you ready, Dad?"

"Almost," he shouted. "Come in. The door's open."

She went in and walked over to the window. "I told that dumb kid to have the taxi here at quarter to ten," she said. "Where's Carole?"

"She called to say she was just about ready and to meet her downstairs."

Donna could see Harry in the bathroom, carefully adjusting the collar of his turtleneck. He turned left and right in front of the mirror, admiring his new fisherman's sweater. She was wearing a Fair Isle sweater over a red turtleneck. They both wore pressed khaki slacks and low-cut boots with rubber soles.

"Have you got your rain jacket?" she asked, looking out the window. "It looks nasty out there." She picked up a piece of toast from Harry's room service tray and took a bite. "What a depressing place. Who in their right mind would want to live here?"

He emerged from the bathroom and pulled a bright yellow rain slicker out of the closet. "Didn't you notice the views when we were flying in yesterday? That's what people want, honey. Scenery, trees, wild animals, that kind of thing."

"That's what you keep saying. I hope you're right." Donna zipped up her jacket and picked up the old shoulder bag stuffed with papers that she had dropped on the bed. Her alligator purse was safely locked in her suitcase, awaiting its journey back to civilization.

Downstairs, Steve paced back and forth in the lobby, waiting for them to come down. He had gotten there half an hour early, even though he had been driving people home from the Snowshoe until two in the morning. Keith had said he'd take over, but Steve had said no. He wanted to find out what was going on.

When they stepped out of the elevator, he smiled and waved. "Hope you had a good night. I hear the beds here are real comfortable."

Donna looked at him and pushed a stray wisp of hair back under her red headband. "The beds were all right, but there was a hell of a noise coming from somewhere down the block. Music, shouting, breaking glass. I had to shut the window and couldn't get any fresh air."

"That's too bad. I can't think where that would have been coming from. It's pretty quiet around here."

"I called the front desk," Harry said, checking his watch, "and they apologized. They said there's a disreputable bar called the Snowshoe down the street that causes a lot of trouble. I wonder where Carole is."

The elevator opened and Carole stepped out in her pink pantsuit topped with a white faux fur vest. "Here I am!" she said, looking at Harry and Donna. "You won't need those rain slickers. It's overcast, but it's not going to rain, is it Steve?"

"I don't think so, Mrs. Riversen. Everybody ready?" He led the way out to the waiting taxi, got them all into their seats, then climbed in and pumped the gas pedal up and down until the engine started. Clouds of white smoke billowed out of the tailpipe. "She's still kinda cold this morning," he said, glancing sideways at Harry.

"We were just talking about the noise coming from that bar down the street last night," Harry said, twisting to look over his shoulder at Carole.

"Oh really, I didn't hear a thing."

Donna looked at her father. "We need to find out more about that place. See how long a lease they've got and if they're breaking any laws."

Steve waited to see if Harry was going to say anything, but he didn't, so he asked, "Where can I take you?"

"Down to the cannery," Carole answered. "I'm taking my friends to meet Jeff and get a tour. I haven't seen the place in years, and I'm curious to see what he's done with it."

They pulled out of the driveway, turned right, and headed toward the water. Steve was hoping they'd say more, but everyone had clammed up. Harry had put his sunglasses on and was looking out the window, Donna was reading some papers she had taken out of her bag, and Carole was checking her makeup in her compact mirror.

Jeff opened the office door and stepped outside when he saw the taxi pull up to the gate. He hadn't been sleeping well and had already had three cups of Sammy's strong black coffee. He walked over to greet the little group as they climbed out of the car.

"Darling!" his mother cried, wobbling through the loose gravel in her high-heeled boots.

"Hi, Mom," he said, embracing her and coughing as a cloud of her familiar perfume hit his lungs. "How was the trip?"

"Oh, no worse than usual. Let me introduce my friends." She turned and pulled Harry forward by the hand. "Harry, I'd like you to meet my son, Jeff."

Harry smiled. "I've heard great things about you. Your mother is very proud of you, young man."

"Thanks. Nice to meet you." They shook hands.

"And this is Donna," Carole added. "Harry's daughter. She works with him on all of his projects."

Jeff looked at the young woman who stepped forward from behind Harry. She stuck her hand out and squeezed his hand, holding it a bit too long before dropping it. Her wide, tight smile made him think she wasn't accustomed to smiling very often.

"I'd know you anywhere," Harry said. "You look a lot like your mother."

"So I've been told," Jeff replied, leading them toward the bunkhouse kitchen. "Let's go inside where it's warm. There are some other people waiting to meet you."

As they entered, Sammy turned to look at them from the back counter where he was cutting coffee cake. Steam wafted from the coffee urn. Artie and John, who were sitting at a table with mugs of coffee, stood up. All three of them wore freshly laundered blue coveralls and clean, new Cove Packers caps. Jeff had put on his best jeans, a new plaid shirt, and a brown leather vest no one had seen before.

After he had introduced everyone, and they had all had cake and coffee, Jeff noticed that Artie was fidgeting in his seat and starting to look annoyed. Harry's small talk about the weather and sailing was of no interest to him. Jeff knew he'd rather be at home, not wasting time with this suntanned outsider. Donna hadn't said much, but he didn't like the way she was staring at him.

"I'm sure you want to get moving and see the place," he said, standing up. "Artie, John, are you ready? It's too bad you couldn't come up when we were busy. It's going to be hard to show you how things work with everything shut down." He opened the kitchen door. "I expect you've seen other small operations like ours. It's old, but not much different from the rest."

Artie frowned, and John raised his eyebrows as they followed Harry, Donna, and Carole out the door. Glancing back, Jeff saw Sammy look at him and shake his head.

"I take it you own all of this," Harry said. "No long-term leases or partners?"

"No. I own it all," Jeff answered. They were standing on the dock behind the slime house, looking at the spot where the beach gang unloaded boats during the season.

"What about loans? How much do you owe the bank?"

"Nothing. I paid off the last of the debt last year."

"Excellent. And how much land is there altogether?"

"About twelve acres. A lot of it's empty, out behind the bunkhouse."

"Why do you need a bunkhouse?" Donna asked. "Wouldn't it be cheaper not to house and feed anyone? It seems to me they could pay for their own food and lodging in town and work a night shift when they were needed."

Jeff looked out at the gray water and the mountains in the distance. There was more snow accumulating on them every week. "This work is dangerous and exhausting," he explained. "The guys need to trust each other and work together in a way I don't think they would if they lived in town on their own."

"Do you live here too?" she asked. "I didn't see a house anywhere."

"I've got an apartment over the office."

"We'll need to see that too, since we're here to make an offer on the whole place."

Jeff looked at her in surprise. It hadn't occurred to him that they'd expect to see every inch of the place. Carole stepped between them and took his arm. "Let's keep moving. We haven't really seen anything yet."

They had scrubbed the slime house so well that only a hint of fish lingered in the cold air. The gray concrete floor was bone dry, and every trace of fish blood had been scoured out of the sinks. The storeroom was tidy and organized. Boxes of gloves and other supplies were stacked in neat rows, waiting for the next season to begin. As they passed the open door, Jeff fought back a wave of anger. An image he had created in his mind of Paul attacking Willow flashed in front of his eyes every time he went near that room.

"So, this is where the salmon are cleaned," Harry said, looking at the old conveyor and the deep sinks. "It's hard to believe people do this for a living, isn't it?"

"God, what a miserable job," Donna said, gazing around and shuddering. "I can't think of anything worse."

"I wonder if there isn't a modern machine that could do all of this. Let's research that, honey." Harry looked at Jeff. "You've done a fine job keeping this old place afloat, but it's going to take a lot of cash to bring it up to modern standards. We have to take that into account when we sit down to talk terms."

Artie, who hadn't said a word so far, pulled his hands out of his coverall pockets and waved at one of the motors. "With the right care, this equipment could last another thirty years. There's nothing wrong with it."

John added, "And Artie has given all of it the best care. You can count on it."

Donna looked at the two of them for a moment, then turned away, saying, "I didn't realize we were buying a museum, Dad."

Jeff led Carole, Harry, and Donna up the stairs to the apartment. After inspecting the slime house, the canning line, the warehouse, and the bunkhouse, they had dropped Artie and John off in the kitchen with Sammy. Harry had asked a few questions along the way and made more remarks about the age of everything. Donna had asked if anyone really ate canned salmon anymore. She clearly did not.

He unlocked the door reluctantly, feeling there was no real need for them to view his private living space. Sammy, he could tell, had felt just as violated when they had traipsed through his bedroom behind the kitchen a few minutes earlier.

"Who's Willow?" Donna asked, looking at the names and wreath of forget-me-nots painted on the door. "Are you married?"

They stepped into the cramped but tidy living room. "No. She's my girlfriend," Jeff answered.

"You know, I don't believe I've been in here since your grandfather passed away," Carole said. She looked at Harry. "My late father-in-law lived here for years." She turned to Jeff. "Where on earth did you sleep when he was still alive? There isn't room to swing a cat in here."

"Sometimes in here on Grandpa's old sofa and sometimes in the bunkhouse."

Carole wrinkled her nose. "I should have made you move to Seattle with us."

Donna crossed the room, glanced in the tiny kitchen, then went into the bedroom. She stared at the brass bed and handmade blue and lavender quilts for a minute, then asked, "Where's your girlfriend now?"

"In London."

"Why? Is she English?"

"No. She's in school, but she'll be back in December."

Carole looked at Jeff. "Oh, that reminds me of something I wanted to tell you, dear. I had coffee with Florence yesterday, and she said Willow might stay in London after her program ends. Apparently, she's been writing to a young man named Alex and has invited him to come over there in a few weeks to discuss a book he's written and wants her to illustrate. Florence seemed to think they would stay over there until it was finished."

"Who's Florence?" Donna asked.

"My girlfriend's mother," Jeff replied, not allowing any emotion to cross his face. He was determined not to give his mother the satisfaction of thinking she had upset him.

Harry looked at his watch. "I think we've seen all we need to see here. Let's call that kid with the taxi and get back to town. Remember, we have an appointment with a real estate agent to see your lake property in an hour, Carole."

She smiled at him and put her arm through his, saying, "Yes, let's get going. I hadn't realized how late it was. Help me down those rickety old stairs, Harry. I'm sure I'll fall without you."

Donna stayed behind, not following them to the door. She looked up at Jeff and put a hand on his chest. "Why don't you come over to the Inn tonight at about ten? We can have a drink in the bar and talk about this deal some more."

Chapter 21

Willow leaned forward and pushed her hands deeper into her raincoat pockets as she hurried down Wigmore Street. The sharp October wind seemed to be blowing from every direction at once, kicking up dead leaves and debris. She was wearing a heavy wool sweater, a long wool skirt, and knee-high lace up leather boots, and was wishing she had put on a warmer coat. When she reached Regent Street, she turned right and started down it.

It was a long walk to Maiden Lane from her room in the attic of her landlady's house, but she had never felt comfortable on the Tube, especially since the IRA bombings in London had become more frequent. There had been two only a few weeks earlier, on Oxford Street and in Sloane Square. The thought of being trapped underground if a bomb went off terrified her.

When she got to Great Marlborough Street, she looked at her watch and decided that she just barely had time to take a quick detour through Liberty's, her favorite store in London. She couldn't afford much of anything in there, but the fabrics and the Tudor

Revival building, constructed from the timbers of two great wooden ships, were endlessly fascinating. She dreamed of being able to pull down bolt after bolt of the finely printed cotton and buy enough of it to make a new quilt.

She'd come back in November and buy a couple of tea towels for her mother for Christmas, she thought, stepping back onto Regent Street after a dash through the store. It made her sad to think about the joy Florence would get from anything that came from London.

Farther down the street, she stopped to look in the windows at Hamleys. She wanted to go in and see if they had any dollhouses or miniatures, but there wasn't time. She'd need to walk much faster and stop looking in windows if she was going to get to Rules by one.

When she finally got to the restaurant, her cheeks pink from the wind and her long, blond braid somewhat the worse for wear, Alex Cooper was already waiting outside. He smiled and took her icy hand, saying, "Happy birthday! I'm so glad you came."

She had been trying not to think about her birthday. She had gotten up early, expecting a long-distance call from Jeff, but it had never come. He always called in the morning on her birthday, before he went to bed in Alaska, but the phone in her landlady's front hall had not rung. "How did you know it was my birthday?" she asked.

"Your mother told me. I stopped to see her before I left."

"I can't believe you quit like that, in the middle of the week, with no notice. What happened?"

"Let's go inside and I'll tell you."

Willow looked around the dining room. She had never seen anything like it. The red velvet banquettes were older, but not all that different from the gold ones in the Beluga Room, but the stained-glass ceiling and dozens of paintings and drawings lining the walls were astonishing. It would take hours to look at everything, and even then she thought she would probably miss half of it.

She turned her attention to the menu. Venison would probably taste a lot like moose, she imagined, and she couldn't even think about salmon. Red partridge sounded nice. Or perhaps duck. Her father hadn't gotten any, so there wouldn't be duck at Christmas unless a friend gave them some. She thought of Jack in Valdez and wondered if he was happy that he hadn't had to go hunting with their father this year.

"I'll have the duck, please," she said to the waiter.

"And partridge for me," Alex said. He looked at Willow. "Save room for dessert. Mother says they make great sponge pudding."

"Have you eaten here before?"

"No, but my English relatives talk about it all the time. It's their favorite place to go for special occasions."

"When was the last time you were over here?"

"Mother and I were here for two months when I was fourteen. That's when I decided I'd find a way to move here permanently. I feel more at home here than I do in Seattle, even though I was born there."

"Does your mother want to move back too?"

"Not really. She fell in love with Seattle after she married my father and went home with him."

"My mother would move back in a heartbeat if she could."

"She might have felt differently if she'd gone to Seattle instead of Agate Cove."

"Maybe." Willow had ordered hot tea because she was so cold, even though she knew it wasn't quite correct. All around them, waiters were opening wine bottles and filling glasses. She picked up her cup and said, "Okay, now tell me what happened."

The waiter came back and set a glass of dry sherry in front of Alex. He took a sip. "Well, things started out all right. I took your advice and asked my students to write an essay about their summer jobs instead of their summer vacations."

"How did that go?"

"It was an eye-opener. I couldn't believe all the dirty, dangerous things those kids were doing. And the hours were shocking. Most of them were working seven days a week, mainly for their parents."

"That's the way it is in summer. Things have to get done."

"They were flying, shooting, fishing, fixing things, building things, at all hours of the day and night, the girls as well as the boys."

"Yeah, so that assignment went well. What next?"

"I decided we'd do a unit on *Hamlet*. I knew most of them wouldn't be able to get through it, so we watched a movie and read some passages, and then I explained the rest and asked them to write an essay about young people having conflicts with their parents."

Willow raised her eyebrows. "And?"

"And that's when I started to find out about the bad stuff going on in Agate Cove. You wouldn't believe how many of those kids were being raised by alcoholics or had parents who hit them. And I won't mention some things a few of the girls wrote about."

"You never had kids like that in your school in Seattle?"

"It was an elite private school. If that kind of thing was going on, I never heard about it."

The waiter arrived with their food. Willow had never tasted such delicious, tender duck before. They ate in silence for a few minutes, then she said, "There are a lot of great people in Agate Cove, but some families have real problems, just like anywhere."

Alex took a bite of partridge. "I tried to talk to the principal, but he said it wasn't my business to ask the students about their troubles at home. He said I should stick to the curriculum and do my job. Things went downhill from there."

"What do you mean?"

"I started feeling sorry for the kids who had the biggest problems, so I stopped expecting them to do their homework or stay awake in class. Pretty soon, almost everyone quit doing the assignments, and my classroom got a reputation for being a place to sleep and socialize. I spent most of my time sitting at my desk, writing the book I mentioned in my letter."

Willow stared at him. She had expected things to go badly, but not quite that badly. "Did the principal find out?"

"Yes. Eventually. A couple of parents came to school and complained, so he barged into the classroom one afternoon, saw what was going on, and we agreed that I should leave and let someone else take over."

"Did you go back to Seattle?"

"Just long enough to sort a few things out and spend a few days with Mother." He paused to swallow the last of his sherry. "I knew after the first week in Agate Cove that I'd never last until Christmas. I was planning to come over here after Thanksgiving, so I'm just a little ahead of schedule."

"I thought you wanted to get enough material for a book about teaching in Alaska."

He laughed. "As soon as I read those summer job essays, I gave up on that idea. I realized I didn't belong there and anything I had to say would sound naïve or stupid, or both."

After their plates had been cleared, they ordered one golden syrup sponge pudding to share. When it arrived, with two forks and spoons, Alex said, "It's not birthday cake, but why don't you make a wish anyway, before we dig in?"

"Okay." Willow closed her eyes, thought for a moment, then opened them. "Done." She picked up her fork. "Are you going to tell me about the book you actually did write, and what you meant by needing my help?"

"I got the idea from the things you told me that day we drove around town. Do you remember? We went to the lake where you learned to swim, and the movie theater, and your grade school?"

"Yeah."

"You had all these little stories about your mother in her funny swim cap and the school skating show. They were charming. So, I started writing a children's book about a little girl growing up in Alaska who did all those things. It took my mind off the teenagers in my class."

"Okay." She took a spoonful of pudding and ate it slowly. "So how do I fit into this?"

"I'd like you to illustrate the book. Your mother showed me some of your drawings one day when I was over there, after you'd left town, and they were wonderful. They were light and playful, just the right style for a children's book."

She stopped eating and thought for a moment. "I don't have time right now. I have a big project to finish at school, and then I'm moving back home. If you're staying here, I don't see how it could work."

"Why don't you just stay here a little longer? How long would it take? A few months, maybe less, right? I have some savings. I could help pay your rent."

"I don't know. I was looking forward to getting home for Christmas."

"Will you at least think about it?"

"All right."

Alex picked up the check, paid the bill, and helped her on with her coat. Outside, they began walking in the general direction of Leicester Square. "You don't seem to be very happy, even though it's your birthday," he remarked. "Do you have any plans for this evening? We could go to the theater."

"Thanks," Willow said, keeping her eyes on the sidewalk, "but I should stay in and work on my project. You're right. I'm not very happy."

"Care to tell me why?"

"I thought my boyfriend would call this morning, but he didn't. He's never forgotten my birthday before."

Alex stopped. "Wait a minute," he said. Willow stopped and turned to look at him. "Your mother told me you two had broken up. She said he was seeing some girl from Seattle whose father is buying the cannery. I didn't want to mention it because I thought it might still be bothering you."

"What? What are you talking about?" Willow felt tears well up in her eyes and begin rolling slowly down her cheeks. She felt as if she were fixed to the sidewalk, as frozen and mute as a statue.

Alex stepped forward and put his arms around her.

Jeff woke with a start and sat up in bed. Drops of icy water were dripping from the ceiling onto his face. The quilts were already cold and soggy on Willow's side of the bed. He cursed, pushed the covers off, and stood up, rubbing his wet hair. He went over to the bedroom window and looked out. A thick layer of heavy, wet snow had fallen during the night, blanketing everything.

He had only slept a few hours and had spent most of the night lying on his back in the dark, wondering what the hell was going on. It was Willow's birthday and he had tried to call her the night before, when it was morning in London, so that he could be the first to wish her happy birthday. He had gotten a busy signal, but kept trying until, at two thirty in the morning Alaska time, her landlady had finally answered. Willow had gone out for the day with Alex, she'd said, and wasn't expected back until midnight at least. "No," she had said, "she didn't leave a message for you."

He got dressed and waded through the snow to the bunkhouse, where Sammy was already frying eggs and bacon. A pot of hot coffee sat on the back of the stove. Since only the two of them were there now, there was no need to fill the big urn. He stomped the snow off his boots and hung up his parka. "There's a damn leak in the roof right over my bed," he said, pouring a cup of coffee.

Sammy looked at him. "I been upstairs and there's leaks in the bunkroom too. I put some buckets out."

"Let's eat and then we'll go take a look around. See what else is falling apart."

They ate in silence, listening to the news on Sammy's portable radio, then bundled up and trudged over to the cannery building. Everything looked dry and still until they got to the warehouse, where a part of the roof had caved in. Wet snow had saturated a tall stack of pallets holding new cardboard boxes, and a wide puddle had formed under some empty gondolas.

Jeff looked at the mess and rubbed his face. "Shit!" he exclaimed. Turning to Sammy, he said, "I'm gonna get the forklift and move stuff out from under that hole. You go call John, okay? Tell him to get down here as soon as he can."

Chapter 22

"All right, Mom, you win. It's bedtime and I'm sick of arguing with you about it. I'll come down the Monday after Thanksgiving, but I'm only staying till Thursday." Jeff leaned back in his office chair. "No, I don't want to have Thanksgiving with Harry and Donna. He's trying to screw me financially and she's trying to screw me the other way. I don't want to go to their house and eat turkey with them."

He hung up and pulled a stack of repair estimates out of the desk drawer. They were all enormous, more than he could pay without borrowing money, and insurance wasn't going to help much. The structural engineer had said no one could work in the cannery or sleep in the bunkhouse if the roofs weren't brought up to code. He had found areas over the canning line and the can shop that might cave in at any moment, just like what had already happened in the warehouse. It wasn't any consolation that the roof over the apartment only needed a small patch. Jeff had already climbed up there and done that himself.

He put the estimates back in the drawer, closed it, and went upstairs. The quilts that had gotten soaked when the roof leaked were still draped around the living room. He touched one of them to see if it was dry enough to go back on the bed and thought of Willow sewing all those fabric scraps together with tiny stitches. The edges were still damp, so he went in the bedroom, took off his boots, jeans, and sweatshirt, and climbed into the sleeping bag he had thrown on top of the sheets.

"You realize, I hope, that we're going to have to reconsider our offer in light of this new information." Harry looked at Jeff across the conference table and smiled. "It doesn't mean we aren't interested, but the numbers will have to change."

"Did you bring the estimates?" Donna asked.

Jeff opened the sleek, black briefcase his mother had pulled out of her closet that morning. It was the only thing she had saved of his father's. Everything else had been destroyed in the plane crash, been sold, or been given to charity. He couldn't believe he was sitting in an office in Seattle using it.

He pushed the estimates across the table, trying not to meet her eye. She had been calling and writing ever since they'd had a drink together that night in the bar at the Agate Inn. He'd gone there against his better judgment, hoping to find out what they were really planning to do with the cannery and his mother's property. All he'd gotten out of it were some strange looks from Steve and the bartender and a lot of aggravation. Donna had already had more than a few drinks by the time he got there and had no intention of discussing business.

She read the estimates, then handed them to Harry. He put on his reading glasses and studied them in silence.

"This is a lot of money," he said, pushing them back across the table to Jeff. "We're going to have to think about it and get back to you in a week or two with a new offer."

Jeff gathered up the papers and put them back in the briefcase. "I understand," he said, pushing his chair away from the table and standing up. "I'm looking into borrowing money for the repairs from a local bank. They're going over the numbers now."

Harry stood up. "Do you really want to go through all that? Wouldn't you rather get a fair price for the old place and let us deal with it? You'll have a nice nest egg and get a monkey off your back at the same time."

"I still don't understand why you're interested in any of it."

Harry picked up his gold fountain pen and put it in his shirt pocket. "I've been investing in all sorts of things since before you were born," he said, "but I've never bought anything in Alaska.

When I met your mother and heard about Agate Cove, I decided it was about time I got a little piece of your beautiful state. Don't worry. We'll get everything fixed up and running like clockwork in no time."

"What about the people who work for me? Will you keep them on?"

"I can't make any promises, but we'll do what we can. Let's not get ahead of ourselves. The way things stand now, you can't even open the place, and that won't help anybody."

Donna stood up and stretched, then bent over to smooth a wrinkle out of her skirt, making sure Jeff could see most of the way down her silk blouse. "Think about it," she said, straightening up, "you'll have more than enough money to buy a decent place to live. I could take you out this afternoon to look at some new condos they're building downtown."

"Even if I agree to sell," Jeff said, taking his coat off the back of a chair, "I don't know that I'd leave Agate Cove."

She pulled a tube of lip gloss out of her bag and ran it over her lips. "Sorry, I guess I misunderstood. Your mother said your girlfriend was seeing someone else now and staying in London, so I assumed you'd want a change of scene."

It was drizzling and completely dark when Willow ran up the steps to the front door and turned her key in the lock. From the chilly, unlit entrance hall she heard the sound of a television coming from the lounge. She glanced into the room, but didn't see Barbara, her landlady. Her cat, Ginger, was sleeping on an overstuffed dark green chair in front of the set. One tiny lamp with a frilly shade, the sort of small, decorative thing that would look more at home on a boudoir dressing table, gave out a feeble light.

"Is that you, dear?" Barbara called from the kitchen at the back of the house.

"Yes," Willow answered. "I'm back."

"I'm just making a cup of tea. Would you like one?"

"Yes, please. Thank you." She took off her coat and hung it on the rack near the door, then went through the lounge to the kitchen. Barbara, a thin woman with gray hair and gray-green eyes who had been a great friend of her mother's during the war, was spooning loose tea into a china pot.

Like Florence, she had married an American serviceman and had a child, a daughter, but her husband hadn't taken her and the baby home to the States as he had promised. In fact, he hadn't taken them anywhere, but had gone back alone and disappeared. She had eventually gotten a divorce and moved on, raising her daughter alone and working for an elderly doctor in Harley Street. Her savings and an inheritance had allowed her to buy a small house with an extra bedroom in the attic which she usually had rented out to a female student from the art school nearby. Her daughter, Anne, lived in Cambridge, so Barbara and Willow were usually alone in the house.

Barbara looked up. "How was your day? Is it raining again?"

"Just drizzling. I'm tired. School was freezing."

"We all have to do our bit to save energy," Barbara said, tearing open a package of Garibaldi biscuits and putting several on a plate. "Would you like a biscuit with your tea?"

"No, thanks. I had a sausage roll and a flapjack in the canteen."

Barbara handed Willow a cup of tea and put her own on a tray with the plate of biscuits. "Would you like to watch telly with Ginger and me?"

"I'd like to, but I can't. I have a lot of work to do. I'll just take my tea upstairs."

"As you wish, dear. Mind the stairs. I put some lamps away and took lightbulbs out of others this afternoon. The news is so grim."

Willow took a sip of tea. "We keep our coats on in class now," she said. "I feel sorry for the models. You can hear their teeth chattering and see them shivering while we draw."

"Poor things." Barbara picked up the tray. "They're calling this is an energy crisis, but things were much worse during the war. We'll get through it. We always do." She led the way to the lounge and pushed the cat off her chair with one hand.

"Was there any mail for me?" Willow asked.

"Yes, a letter from your mother. I put it in your room."

"Okay. Thanks." She went back into the dark hall and headed for the stairs.

"I'll make you a hot water bottle at bedtime," Barbara called from the lounge. She set the tray on a small table next to her chair and wrapped a tartan wool blanket around her knees. Ginger jumped onto her lap, turned around a couple of times, and went back to sleep.

On the landing at the top of the stairs, Willow saw that Barbara had indeed been busy. The bulbs in the wall sconces were missing, and a large lamp that usually sat on an oak table had vanished. In its place was a mate to the boudoir lamp she had just seen in the lounge, giving off a soft, anemic glow through its ruffled, lavender shade.

Barbara had been saying they had to do more, that things would only get worse as the winter wore on. All across Europe and the United Kingdom people were being told to conserve energy, to darken their streets, shops, and homes, and get used to being cold.

She crossed the landing and started up the attic stairs. They were steep, uncarpeted, and well-worn from decades of use. The handrail was thin, shaky, and not well-anchored to the wall. As she climbed up to her room, she wished she had a flashlight. The little boudoir lamp on the table below only illuminated the first few steps. After that, she used the toes of her boots to feel her way up to the top.

She got to her room at last and ran her hand along the wall, feeling for the old-fashioned light switch. When she finally found it and pushed, nothing happened. Barbara had removed the bulb from the ceiling fixture. Willow sighed and felt her way to her desk where, fortunately, her desk lamp was still in place and still functioning. Her mother's letter sat next to it.

The room was cold, but not as cold as she had expected. Barbara had probably turned the central heating on when she was going through the house removing lightbulbs, but that had been several hours earlier. It wouldn't come on again until the next day. Willow sat down and opened the letter.

It was full of news about Jack being home from Valdez for Thanksgiving and the house projects he had done with her father during the week he was there, but the only part she cared about was on the last page. Jeff, Florence reported, had been invited to their house for Thanksgiving, as usual, but had refused, saying he had other plans. And then Jack had run into Steve one evening in the Snowshoe and Steve had told him he'd seen Jeff drinking at the Inn with a girl named Donna from Seattle. What's more, Steve said, John and Artie had told him Donna and her father were buying the cannery and Jeff was going to Seattle the week after Thanksgiving to sign the papers. Everyone in town was talking about it.

She put the letter down and stared blankly at the folder holding her unfinished final project. It was almost done, but now she didn't know if she would ever finish it. She didn't even care. Jeff hadn't called or written since the week before her birthday, and she hadn't written to him either. If her family and Alex and all of Agate Cove knew what he was doing, why didn't he have the guts to tell her himself? She couldn't believe what was happening.

She pulled an unfinished drawing forward from the back of the desk. It was a bigger version of the quick sketch of a squirrel she had made in July at the old mine. The scrap of paper she had found to draw on in Jeff's truck was on top of the new drawing. She picked it up and felt the memory of that day and all the others like it overwhelm her as she ripped it into tiny bits and dropped them in the wastebasket.

Her tea was stone cold, and the drizzle had turned into a heavy rain that pounded against her bedroom window. She pushed her chair back and stood up, thinking she'd go downstairs and make a fresh cup in the kitchen.

At the top of the stairs, laughter drifted up from the television two floors below. Barbara was losing her hearing and kept the volume at a level that hurt Willow's ears when they watched something together. Most of the attic steps were dark, but she could see the ones at the bottom, bathed in a dim lavender light from the lamp below. Holding the teacup in her left hand and gripping the handrail with her right, she went down slowly. On the third step, the loose rail came away from the wall when she pulled on it. She lost her balance, pitched forward, and fell headfirst down the steep stairs. She heard the sounds of china smashing and someone screaming and wondered if that was her voice or someone else's.

When she tried to open her eyes at the bottom of the stairs, only one would open. The other seemed to be stuck shut. After a moment, she realized that she was sprawled on the landing at the bottom of the attic stairs. Her ribs and her left wrist hurt and she didn't feel like moving. Something seemed to be wrong with her head. The sound of someone rushing up the stairs came from below. She closed the one eye she could open and began to drift off, dreaming that Jeff was leaning over her and shaking her shoulder.

"Oh, my God!" Barbara shouted as she crossed the landing and knelt next to Willow. She shook her shoulder gently. When Willow opened one eye and turned her head slowly toward her, Barbara could see that her other eye was crusted shut with blood coming from a deep, long gash in her scalp that went from the top of her forehead all the way back to the crown of her head, just to the right of her part. She must have hit the top of her head on the sharp edge of the door casing at the bottom of the stairs.

Barbara took her hand and said, "Don't try to move. I'll call the ambulance," and rushed downstairs to the telephone in the hall.

Willow closed her eye again. She didn't feel cold or even particularly uncomfortable there on the floor. In fact, she thought she would just like to sleep for a while.

The next thing she heard was the sound of voices and heavy boots pounding up the stairs. She opened the one eye that wasn't stuck shut and saw a broad-shouldered man in a blue uniform crossing the landing toward her. He knelt down and spoke slowly into her ear.

"We can't get you down those stairs on a stretcher," he said, "so I'm going to carry you down and put you on a stretcher in the front hall. There's an ambulance waiting outside."

Willow looked at him and tried to nod. He reminded her of Jeff. His voice was deep and calm like his, but he was older and bigger. A great bear of a man, in fact, but with the same piercing blue eyes and sandy hair. She closed her eye and felt him carefully lift her up in both arms. His thick, wool uniform itched her face, and she worried that it was being ruined by the blood trickling down her cheek.

When they reached the hall, he placed her gently on the stretcher and buckled the straps around her. He and another man maneuvered it onto the sidewalk. She heard gasps from people who had gathered outside to see what was happening and wondered why they were making those sounds. A woman's voice said, "Is she dead? Just look at all that blood!"

Barbara was there, saying, "These men will take good care of you. I'll get a taxi and see you at the hospital."

"What about my bag? My passport?" Willow whispered.

"Don't worry about a thing, dear. I have them right here."

"Please don't tell my mother. She'll only make things worse."

"I won't. Not right away. But I'll tell Alex. He'll want to see you."

On the way to the hospital, another man sat in back with her and asked questions, doing his best to fill out some forms on a clipboard while they bounced through the wet streets of London.

"What happened?" he asked. "Do you remember?"

"I fell down the stairs. It was dark and I couldn't see the steps," Willow mumbled. She could taste the blood in her mouth and felt it drying on her skin.

"Had you been drinking?"

"No. I don't drink."

"Are you sure."

"I don't drink. Ever."

"Why didn't you turn the light on so you could see the stairs properly?"

"There was no light to turn on. The attic stairs were dark."

"Why were you in the attic in the dark?"

"I live there. I mean, my bedroom is there."

"So, you're accustomed to the stairs being dark?"

"No, they aren't usually dark. My landlady changed the lights today because of the energy crisis." Willow felt her head beginning to throb.

"You sound American or Canadian. Where's your family?" he asked.

"They're in Alaska. My mother is British. I'm going to school here."

"Alaska? Now that's something different." He set his clipboard down on the floor of the ambulance and looked at her more closely. "I'd like to go salmon fishing there one day."

By then Willow had closed her eye again, turned her head away, and gone back to sleep. He shook her arm, saying, "Stay awake, miss. We're almost at the hospital."

Chapter 23

Jeff looked up from his bowl of chicken noodle soup and asked, "Did the mail come yet?"

Sammy was pouring a cup of coffee for himself. "No. Joe ain't been getting down here till after six lately. He says they're short-handed since so many people went off to work on the Line."

Jeff grunted. He hadn't gotten a letter from Willow in six weeks, even though he mailed one to her every Friday afternoon. He'd stopped calling because whenever he did the line was busy, her landlady didn't answer, or, if she did, she told him Willow was out, usually with Alex. He hated not hearing from her, not knowing what was going on. It felt like something he couldn't see had taken control of his life.

When she had been writing, the thin, blue airmail envelopes with the foreign stamps were the first ones he had grabbed when the mail arrived, taking them upstairs to read slowly in the apartment. He always read them again before bed, sometimes falling asleep while reading them and rolling over the crinkly paper in the middle of the night.

There had been snow on the ground for weeks, piling up steadily against the buildings and along the sides of the roads. It was here to stay until breakup came along in the spring. Then it would melt a bit, freeze again, then melt a little more, slowly creating great quagmires of icy mud and exposing half-frozen clods of dirt. Last night had brought new snow, the kind that stuck to shovels and boots and was easy to compress into hard, dense snowballs.

When he was a kid, Jeff and his friends loved that kind of snow. They built forts behind the house and had vicious snowball fights that left them red-faced and sopping wet. As an adult, he couldn't stand the stuff and longed for light, powdery snow that could be brushed away. He knew the temporary patches on the roofs wouldn't stand up to too much of this wet crap.

"All right," he said, finishing his soup and handing the empty bowl to Sammy. "I've got stuff to do in the office. We can watch TV tonight if you want. I got the set working again."

"Maybe," Sammy answered, "but I got that western from the library to finish by Friday. I already checked it out three times in a row, and the librarian says I gotta let someone else have a turn."

Jeff poured himself a cup of coffee and went next door. It was just after one, but not very light outside. A thick layer of clouds threatened more snow before the sun set in three hours. He sat down at the desk, opened a drawer, and pulled out the latest offer from Harry and Donna. The first one had been an insult, and this one was a lot lower. Not only had they pointed out how much it would cost to repair the roofs and modernize the equipment, but they were now saying that freezer plants were going to make salmon canneries obsolete. The market for canned salmon was going to collapse in the next couple of years, they predicted. Everyone wanted fresh, or at least fresh frozen salmon, not something out of a can. They implied that if he didn't take their offer, he'd never get one from anyone else and might go bankrupt.

He'd think about it until Monday, he decided. That was four days away, and then he'd call Harry and accept the offer if he hadn't come up with any better ideas. The roofs had to repaired, and the money for that had to come from somewhere. The guys at the bank had looked at his books and said they were impressed, considering the state things were in when his grandfather died, but the whole proposition wasn't solid enough to justify a big loan. They had advised him to take Harry's offer and be glad someone with deep pockets was willing to put money into the old place.

The phone rang, startling him. He hoped it would be Willow, even though she had never called from London before. He waited until the third ring before answering it.

"Cove Packers."

"It's me, honey, and I've got big news." His mother sounded so excited, she was almost breathless. "We're flying up there next Wednesday. Can you believe it? Me, back in Agate Cove twice in just a few months. I had to go to Frederick's and buy new winter clothes for the trip."

"What are you talking about?" Jeff asked, shoving the papers back in a drawer. "I got Harry's new offer a few days ago, and I'm thinking about it. Don't waste your time coming up here to twist my arm."

"Not me and Harry. Me and Bill. But you can't tell Harry. Or Donna."

"Who's Bill?"

"Don't you ever read my letters? Bill Scott. He's one of my neighbors. I told you about his house and the big party he had in September. Between you and me, I think he might turn out to be 'the one.' We've been seeing a lot of each other."

Jeff thought about it for a few minutes. He vaguely remembered something she'd written about dancing barefoot and a huge house on the water. He hadn't paid much attention. "Why are you coming here with him? It sounds crazy. Have you been drinking?"

"Of course not. I've only had one highball. Anyway, it's almost cocktail time here. Now listen, Bill told me to tell you not to accept

Harry's offer or even talk to him until we get there and he's had a chance to sit down and talk to you himself."

"Why? What's he got to do with it?"

"He wouldn't tell me the details, but I think he's going to come up with a better offer than Harry's. I've been telling him all about it, and you wouldn't believe how interested he is."

"That doesn't make any sense. The bank told me yesterday that the whole thing is likely to go belly-up in a year or two, and now you've come up with two fools who want to buy it."

"They aren't fools, honey. Both of them have more money than you can imagine and know everything about business. I'm pretty sure Bill has even more than Harry."

"I don't know what the hell's going on with anything anymore. Sure, come on up. You're going to hate it. The snow's up to your knees."

Carole was silent for a moment. "I got new boots. And a cute coat with fur trim. Bill says I look like Susie in it."

"Look, Mom, I'm busy. Go ahead and bring this guy up here. At this point, I'll talk to anyone."

"You mean you're finally willing to sell and move out of there? That's the best news I've had all year. Does that mean you're not seeing Willow anymore? I told you she was running off with that writer."

Jeff ran his hand through his hair and looked out the office window. "Mom, I don't know. I haven't heard from her in a while, that's all."

"She's not your type. I always said that, but you wouldn't listen. She's artsy and you're not. A penniless writer will be perfect for her."

"Stay out of it, Mom."

Jeff heard ice clinking in a glass on the other end of the line, then Carole said, "Don't feel bad for one minute, honey. Bill and I will find just the right girl for you. He knows absolutely everyone worth knowing in Seattle."

"I'm going to hang up now."

"Now promise you won't breathe a word to Harry before we get there."

Jeff put the phone down, then ran upstairs to the apartment and threw himself face down on the bed.

Half an hour later, he heard the phone ringing again in the office. He got up, pushed his hair out of his eyes, and went down to answer it.

"Cove Packers," he mumbled, still groggy from his brief nap.

"Jeff, is that you?"

"Florence? Is something wrong? Is Willow okay?" He felt his stomach tighten.

"Jeff, can you come over right away? It's Jim. I don't know what to do."

"What's wrong? Slow down. What's wrong with Jim?"

"He's just lying there!" she wailed. "Just lying out there in the snow! I can't wake him up. He said he wouldn't pay Keith a dime to plow the driveway." She gulped. "He said he'd shovel it himself and be done by two. I told him not to. I told him not to." She was sobbing now.

"Florence, listen to me. You've got to call the ambulance. Have you done that?"

"No," she whispered. "There's no reason to call them. He's gone. I know he's gone. I saw so many dead bodies in London during the war. I know what dead people look like."

"I'll call them," Jeff said. "You stay with Jim. I'll be there in a few minutes."

After the ambulance, police, and other attendants of death had driven away into the fading afternoon light, taking the mortal remains of Jim Marsh with them, Jeff stood alone in the deserted driveway. Snow was falling again, and the Marsh home, deep in the silent woods, felt as isolated as any remote homestead in the bush, even though it was not far from the grade school where they had all learned to read and skate.

Those days seemed so long ago now. He bent over and picked up the snow shovel Jim had been using before his heart gave out, sending him face down into the wet snow. It needed to be dried and put back in the shed. He'd do that, and then he'd call Keith and ask him to come over and clear the driveway in the morning.

A few minutes later, when he entered the house through the back door, he found Florence sitting at the kitchen table in near darkness. A half empty box of Kleenex and a pile of used tissues littered the table. She turned to look at him.

"What should I do?" she asked. "Jim was the boss. He always told the rest of us what to do."

Jeff turned on the lights, closed the curtains, and sat down across from her at the table. "Can I get you something?" he asked. "A drink? A cup of tea?"

"There's a bottle of raspberry cordial in the cupboard behind you," she said. "I made it for Christmas, but there's no point in saving it now. Would you mind getting it out?"

He found the bottle and poured a little of the ruby liquid into two small glasses. He handed one to Florence, then sat down with his own and took a sip. The syrupy, intense flavor of homegrown raspberries exploded in his mouth, igniting memories of long summer days and light summer nights, of picking raspberries in the garden with Willow late in the evening after the cannery had shut down, of holding her in his arms on an old blanket spread out on the grass, of laughing and eating ripe berries by the handful.

"We need to call Willow and Jack," he said. "What about funeral arrangements? Did you and Jim make any plans?"

"No. He always said we were too young to think about such things. He said we were healthy and active and would live a long time." She set her empty glass on the table. "Jim hated funerals. Whenever we had to go to one he'd say, 'I sure as hell don't want some stranger droning on about me like that.'"

"Are there other relatives? Anyone else we should call?"

"No. Jim was an only child. He grew up in North Dakota, but left to join the service when the war started and never went back. His folks died years ago. It wasn't a happy family. His father was an alcoholic."

Jeff swallowed the last few drops of cordial in his glass. He looked at his watch and stood up. "I'm going to call Jack. He should be able to get here by tomorrow afternoon. Sooner if the roads aren't a mess."

Florence looked up at him. "Please don't call Willow," she said. "I don't want her to come home now. She has to finish her classes, and I told her to stay in London, at least for Christmas. That's more important to me than having her here."

Jeff stared at her, not knowing what to think. "She has to be told, Florence."

"No, not now." She began weeping again and reached for a tissue. "I won't need her if Jack comes home. She absolutely has to stay in London. All I've ever wanted was for her to have a good life in London and not be buried alive here like me. Please don't call her."

Jeff went into the living room and picked up the telephone. "Operator, I need to reach Jack Marsh at the Terminal Camp in Valdez. It's urgent. There's been a death in the family. Yes, I'll wait."

He felt the eyes of Florence's great-grandmother boring into him, silently accusing him of wanting to ruin Willow's life. He had never paid any attention to the painting before, but now she seemed to be staring right at him, demanding to know who he thought he was, a nobody in a nowhere place, trying to lure her beautiful, talented great-great-granddaughter away from London, the place where her own mother knew she'd be happy.

He sat down on the damask-covered chair where Willow had sat all those months ago having tea with Alex and put his head in his hands. He felt like a chasm had opened under his feet and his past, present, and future were sliding into it.

The telephone receiver on the desk suddenly crackled and Jeff heard Jack's voice saying, "Hello? This is Jack Marsh."

He picked up the phone. "Jack? It's Jeff." There was a terrible echo on the line. "You need to come home. It's your father. He had a heart attack and passed away this afternoon. Your mother needs you."

There was dead silence. Jeff asked, "Jack, are you there? Can you hear me? Damn this echo!"

"I can hear you." Jack's voice was calm and quiet. "How did it happen? What was he doing?"

"We got a lot of wet snow last night, and he went out to shovel the drive. Your mom found him after lunch."

After another long silence, Jack said, "Idiot. Tell my mother I'm on my way. Thanks, Jeff." The line went dead.

Jeff put the phone down and turned around. Florence was standing in the doorway between the kitchen and the living room. "Is he coming?" she asked.

"Yes. He said to tell you he's on his way."

"Thank God. Things will be better when he gets here. He'll know what to do."

"Do you want me to sleep on the couch tonight? Or call someone? A friend? You might not want to be alone."

He had never thought of Florence as an enemy before. He'd known she wasn't happy in Agate Cove and had pressured Willow to go to school in London, but he never thought she'd do anything to pull them apart. Now he wondered what she and his mother had been up to.

He looked around the snug log home Jim had worked so hard to build for his family. The tools in the shed out back were clean and organized. The freezer was full of moose, and the shelves in the pantry were loaded with delicious things made from the summer's berries and vegetables, yet Florence said she'd been buried alive.

She looked at him as if she sensed his disapproval. "I'll be fine," she said. "There's no need for you to stay any longer. I have a lot to think about. And Jack will be here tomorrow..." Her voice trailed off.

"I'll get going, then. Call me if you change your mind later. I can come over any time." After a moment he added, "I always liked Jim. He was a good man."

She looked at him as if she had forgotten he was still there. "Yes. Yes, he was. A very good man."

Jeff got in his truck and drove slowly back to the cannery with the radio playing softly. The roads were covered in fresh snow. At one point, he passed Keith, who was out working in the dark with his snowplow. *I'll call him tonight*, he thought, *and offer him a big tip to clear the Marsh's driveway before Jack gets home.*

Sammy was playing solitaire at one of the tables in the bunkhouse kitchen when Jeff got back. He looked up and said, "I put your supper in the oven to stay warm. Didn't know where you were or when you were comin' back."

"Thanks. I've been drinking raspberry cordial on an empty stomach. I need some food to settle it down."

Sammy got up and pulled a covered casserole out of the oven. "Now where would you be doin' that? They don't have raspberry cordial at the Snowshoe, so you must have been someplace else."

Jeff sat down. "I was drinking with Florence Marsh. Jim had a heart attack and died this afternoon."

Sammy froze for a moment, then set the hot dish on the counter. "He wasn't that old, was he? What was he doin'?"

"Shoveling snow. Trying to clear that long driveway of theirs by himself."

Sammy spooned pot roast and potatoes onto a plate. "Sounds like Jim. Pigheaded and too cheap to hire any help. Wherever he is now, I bet he's blaming Jack for the whole thing."

"Yeah, I expect so."

"Did you call Willow?"

"No. Florence said not to. I got hold of Jack, and he's coming home tomorrow."

Chapter 24

Willow dipped her smallest paintbrush into a blend of brown watercolor paints and added three final strokes to the squirrel's tail, then dunked the brush in a jar of murky water, swished it around, and sat back in her chair. That was it. Done. Done with the final project, done with school.

She stood up, stretched, and ran her hand through her hair, feeling the fresh, lumpy scar on her scalp. The stitches were gone and clumps of hair next to the long cut had stopped falling out, but it still hurt when she touched it.

After the accident, Barbara had moved Willow's things out of the attic and into her daughter's room on the floor below, and had gotten up every night for two weeks to check on her. They had only argued once: when Barbara had brought a pair of scissors into the bathroom and tried to talk Willow into cutting her hair. A short haircut would make it much easier, she had said, to keep the wound clean, but Willow had refused.

The doorbell chimed downstairs, bringing Barbara out from the kitchen at the back of the house. A moment later, she called up the stairs, "Willow! Alex is here."

"I'll be right down. I have to wash my hands and brush my hair."

"He has some lovely flowers for you."

Willow glanced at the vase of pale pink roses on the corner of her desk. Faded, brown-edged petals were beginning to drop onto her papers. She didn't want to think about how much Alex had spent on out-of-season flowers since her crash down the attic stairs.

She gripped the thick oak banister with both hands and crept sideways down the stairs like a crab, wondering when she would feel confident enough to race up and down them without flashing back on the night she lost her balance and fell headfirst into darkness. Strangely, she had no memory of the moment she hit the door casing, cut her scalp open, and landed on the floor.

When he saw her coming down, Alex crossed the hall to meet her. "Feeling any better?" he asked, a worried frown creasing his forehead.

"Still a bit shaky, to be honest. I hate being afraid of stupid things like going down the stairs. I hope this goes away soon."

"I brought you these," he said, holding out the flowers.

She took the bouquet and smelled the soft white roses. Each one was perfect, only half open, with a delicate hint of pink on the edge of each petal. "They're beautiful," she said, smiling, "but you're spending too much."

"I don't care, not if they make you happy."

Barbara, who had been waiting by the door, came over. "I'll exchange them for the ones in your room," she said, reaching for the flowers. "Put your coat on and go for a walk. You've hardly set foot out of the house."

Alex went over to the coat rack and got Willow's long raincoat. "This one is yours, right?"

"Oh no, that one's too thin for a day like this," Barbara said, "especially since you aren't well. Take mine. I'm not going out this afternoon."

"Are you sure?" Willow replied. "I can go upstairs and get my parka."

"No, no, just wear mine. You shouldn't be going up and down the stairs any more than necessary."

"All right. Thanks. We won't be gone long."

Outside, she and Alex stood under a leafless tree and thought about where to go. Barbara's thick, wool coat was too short for Willow, especially in the sleeves. Her thin wrists jutted out several inches below the itchy, brown cuffs. She looked at her hands and realized they were still stained with ink and paint after days of working on her final portfolio. She showed them to Alex. "Sorry. I'm a mess."

He smiled and tucked her left hand tightly under his arm. "Let's go to Regent's Park."

Her first instinct was to pull away, but she liked the warm, secure feeling of being next to him. Normally, she would have raced alone down the sidewalk with her coat half-buttoned and her hair flying, barely noticing the cheerful, red double-decker buses and chubby black taxis, but today everything seemed menacing and overwhelming. She was happy to lean against his arm and let him lead the way.

After they had walked several blocks, she stopped and looked at him. "I'm really sorry, but the park is still pretty far away, and my ribs are aching. I don't think I can go that far."

"Don't feel bad; I shouldn't have suggested it. Let's head back. Should I get a taxi?"

"No, you've already wasted enough money on me. I can make it back."

"Come here," he said, pulling her up against a black iron railing with trimmed boxwood behind it. "Have you made a decision yet?

Are you going to stay and work on the book with me? I already talked to Barbara, and she said she'd be happy to have you stay."

Willow stared at the ground for a while, then looked up. "I'll stay long enough to do the illustrations, if you can tell me how many and what they should look like by Christmas."

"That's great, but it doesn't give me much time."

"I thought you'd already written the story and were ready to get going."

"I am. I mean, I have written it. I just haven't thought about where the pictures should go. Can I bring it over tonight and read it to you?"

"Sure. How about seven? Barbara and I eat early."

"Why do we need to figure this out before Christmas? That's only a week away."

"I want to work on the drawings over the holidays. I haven't got anything else to do."

Alex took both of her hands in his. "Why don't we do something together? We could go somewhere neither of us has ever been. How about Bath? Or Belgium? We could have an adventure."

"I don't know. So much has happened. I can't think straight."

"You mean with your boyfriend at home?"

"Yeah. I never in a million years thought he'd do this to me. I still can't believe it. And I really can't believe he wouldn't write or call to tell me what he was doing."

Alex pulled her close and put his arms around her. "I'm sorry. I never met him, but your mother didn't think he was good for you. Maybe she was right."

She buried her face in his shoulder and began to cry. "He wasn't good for the person she wants me to be, but he was perfect for who I really am."

He stroked her hair. "Let's try to have some fun over Christmas, and then we'll get to work on the book. I know it's going to be great."

She brushed her eyes with her sleeve. "Okay."

They walked back to Barbara's in silence, Willow clinging tightly to his arm. When they opened the front door and stepped into the hall, Barbara came out of the lounge to meet them. Her expression was careworn, but she seemed to be on edge, as if she had been anxiously awaiting their return. "There you are at last," she said, closing and locking the front door.

"We weren't gone very long, were we?" Willow asked. "Did you need your coat?"

"No, no, nothing like that. Come in here. Both of you," she said, leading them into the lounge and pushing the cat off a small sofa. "Please have a seat."

They sat down and looked expectantly at her. She remained standing, nervously twisting a linen tea towel that had somehow made its way out of the kitchen. "I'm afraid I have bad news," she began, looking directly at Willow. "The phone rang not long after you went out. It was your mother, calling to say that your father had a heart attack two days ago. I'm afraid he didn't survive."

Willow stared at her. "Two days ago? Why didn't she call me then?"

"She knew you were finishing your portfolio, and she didn't want to upset you before you were done. She said to tell you there was nothing anyone could have done."

Alex moved closer to Willow and put his arm around her shoulder.

She looked first at him, then at Barbara, and said, "I have to go home."

"Your mother said I should try to stop you from doing that. She said your brother was with her, and there was no reason for you to come home. They aren't having a funeral. Apparently, your father didn't want one."

Willow stood up. "I can start packing tonight and turn my project in tomorrow. I'll leave the day after that."

Alex looked at her. "What about all the things we were just talking about? What about Belgium? What about the book?"

"I'm sorry. You go to Belgium and send me a postcard. I'll probably never get there, but if I do, there's only one person I want to go with."

"And the book?"

"Why can't I work on it from home? I'm sure we can figure something out."

Alex stood up. "Okay." He hugged her. "I'm really sorry about your dad. Let me know when you're ready to start, and I'll send you my ideas. I'd better get going."

After she had closed the door behind him, Barbara said, "There's something else I have to tell you. Let's go back in the lounge."

"What is it?" Willow asked.

Barbara had finally agreed to sit down. It was getting dark outside, so she reached over and turned on the little lamp with the frilly shade. "I know it was wrong of me, but your mother insisted. She was so convincing."

"What do you mean?" Willow suddenly felt cold, as if the damp fog gathering outside had seeped into her bones.

Barbara looked down at the cat who had jumped into her lap and stroked it nervously. "Your mother said your boyfriend was seeing someone else and not being honest about it. She said she and your father had never trusted him, that he came from a disreputable family, and they needed my help because you were getting too serious about him."

"When was this?"

"Just before you came back here."

"What kind of help did she want?"

"She asked me to tear up his letters and tell him you were away if he called. I wouldn't do it at first, but when you told me Alex was taking you to Rules for your birthday, I thought, 'Why not start now?' Your mum said Alex was a much better match for you, and I should do all I could to encourage him."

Willow clenched her hands together, trying to keep them from shaking. "Did Jeff call on my birthday?"

"Yes. I kept the phone off the hook until you went out. When he called later, I told him you had gone out for the day with Alex."

"How many letters did you destroy?"

"I don't know. At least one a week. They usually came on Thursday, when you were at school. I feel terrible about it."

Willow got up. "I don't know what to say." She began walking out of the room. "I'm glad I'm leaving. And I'm going to call Jeff now. Don't worry, you won't have to pay for it."

"I'm so sorry, dear. Your mother is one of my oldest and dearest friends. I trusted her to know what was best for you."

"All right, Mom, we're all here. What's going on?" Jeff leaned back against the kitchen counter in the bunkhouse kitchen and looked at Carole and Bill. They were seated at one of the tables, drinking coffee. John and Artie were at another table, and Sammy was lurking in the background, opening and closing the oven to check on a batch of butter cookies. Jeff hadn't told him until nine in the morning that everyone would be showing up at ten for a meeting.

Carole looked around the room. "This is my good friend, Bill, and he's got some great news."

Artie set his coffee mug down. "And what would that be?"

Bill scraped his chair back and stood up. "I think you need to know about something that's going to affect all of you. I'm in the travel and cruise business, and it's going to be expanding here in Alaska sooner than you think. Quite a few companies are interested in bringing people to Agate Cove if they can locate the right kind of hotel rooms and other amenities. They're going to need shops, restaurants, tour buses, guides, and a first-rate dock as well.

No one spoke. Finally, Jeff said, "When do you think this might happen?"

"I don't know for sure, but you're going to be hearing a lot about it soon. People are already trying to buy up property and making plans for all the visitors they expect to come up here."

Jeff looked at his mother. "People like Harry Lewis?"

Bill looked down at Carole, then at Jeff. "I'm afraid so. Your mother showed me his latest offer. That's when I felt like I had to say something. He's trying to get her prime lakefront property for a song so he can build a hotel on it, and he wants everything you own down here so he can either sell it off to developers or build a new dock and a bunch of waterfront shops. If you accept his offer, I guarantee he'll have the bulldozers in here before you know it and demolish this place. Then he'll sit on the land until he can do something to make a tidy profit."

John whistled slowly under his breath. Sammy pulled the cookies out of the oven, saying, "I knew he was a crook."

Jeff looked at Bill. "You could have told me this on the phone. Why did you come up here in the dead of winter?"

"Because I wanted to see the place for myself, even if it's not the best time to look at it. And I want to make you an offer that's a hell of a lot better than Harry's and will keep everyone working for as long as possible."

CHAPTER 25

Willow, Jack, and Florence sat at the kitchen table looking at each other. Florence and Jack had cups of black tea with milk in front of them. Willow had a mug of Russian tea. The sweet blend of spices, tea, and Tang tasted delicious after months of drinking Barbara's perfectly brewed, but ultimately unsatisfying, cuppas.

"Why didn't Jeff pick me up at the airport?" she asked.

"I told him not to," Florence answered. "We thought, under the circumstances, that Jack ought to do it. This is a family crisis, after all, and Jeff isn't family."

Willow looked down and said nothing.

"Christmas is in four days," Jack said, looking at his mother. "Should we do anything about it? I mean, get out some decorations or something? Dad always liked having lights on the house."

"That would be nice, putting up some lights for him. I don't care about the rest of it. I've got too much on my mind to think about the holidays."

"I have to go back to Valdez on Boxing Day, so as far as I'm concerned, there's no point in getting everything out. I'll find a few strings of lights and put them up this afternoon."

They both looked at Willow. "What about you, Sis?" Jack asked. "You're the one who always cared the most about the tree and all that stuff."

Willow thought about how happily she and her mother had decorated the tree when she was little. She had loved opening the boxes of ornaments and greeting them like long lost friends. There were miniature Union Jack flags, blown glass apples and pears, sterling silver snowflakes, little embroidered corgis and crowns, porcelain Peter Rabbits, and all sorts of odd things made out of popsicle sticks and felt by Willow and Jack when they were in grade school.

"I don't know," she said at last. "I'm feeling jet-lagged, and my head hurts."

Florence spoke up. "I simply cannot believe that neither you nor Barbara saw fit to tell us about your accident. I just don't understand you sometimes."

"There was nothing you could do. I didn't want to upset you."

Jack looked at her. "You should have told her, Sis."

"And she shouldn't have done all the rotten things she did to me and Jeff. Did you know she told Barbara to tear up his letters?"

"You've been pushing me out of your life ever since you got involved with him," Florence complained. "You used to tell me everything and listen to my advice."

"No, I didn't," Willow said. "There were lots of things I never told you, and I only followed your advice when I wanted to."

"What do you mean? That's not true."

"Mum, I spent most of my time alone when I was growing up, either in the woods or riding my bike around town. You never even noticed when I was gone because you were too busy with all your letters. Your heart was never really here. It was in England."

"That's not fair, Sis," Jack said, taking his empty cup to the sink. "She did a great job raising us and you know it. You're just feeling crappy right now. Let's try to get something done around here instead of arguing."

Willow got up next. "I'm sorry. What do you want us to do, Mum? I can look through the papers on Dad's desk or bag up his clothes for charity if you don't feel up to it. Where do you want to start?"

Florence took her cup to the sink. After rinsing it for a long time, she turned around and said, "I've had a lot of time to think, and there are some things I need to tell you two. Let's go to my room."

She wiped her hands on a kitchen towel, then led them through the living room, down the hall, and into her room, where the old shoeboxes full of letters had been pulled out from under the bed. Some had their lids off. Others had their contents arranged in piles next to them.

Florence gestured toward the bed, saying, "Sit down if you like. This may take a while."

Willow sat down on the pale green bedspread, still clutching her mug with both hands. Jack said, "No thanks. I've been sitting too much already." They looked at Florence.

She picked up a thick bundle of letters with a rubber band around them, one of dozens that looked exactly the same. "You know your father and I were married in London in 1944. Jack was born there a little under eight months later." She paused, looking out the bedroom window at the long icicles hanging down from the eaves. "What you don't know is that I was already pregnant with Jack when we got married."

"That isn't such a big deal today, Mum," Willow said. "I know it was in those days, but things have changed."

"I always knew I was born early," Jack said, "but I thought that was because you were malnourished from the wartime food rationing. That's what you told me once." Jack started to leave the room, but turned and said, "If that's all, I should go look for those lights."

"Wait, that's not all."

He turned around again and looked at her.

"This isn't easy to say, but when I married your father, I had only known him for two weeks. Things like that happened during the war. The baby I was carrying wasn't his, and I didn't tell him I was pregnant."

"What?" Jack came over to the bed and sat down next to Willow.

"Mummy, are you saying Daddy wasn't Jack's father?"

"That's exactly what I'm saying. Now that Dad is gone, I think Jack has a right to know."

Jack looked stunned. Suddenly, he began laughing.

"Do you think this is funny? This is so hard for me, and you're laughing."

Jack got up and hugged her. "No, you don't understand. I'm not laughing at you. Why would I do that? It just explains so much. Why I have red hair when no one else in the family does. Why I never felt connected to the old man and why he probably never felt connected to me. I think we both knew there was something wrong. I've been blaming myself for all of it, and now I can stop."

Willow set her empty mug on the nightstand. "Can you tell us anything about Jack's real father?"

Florence held out the bundle of letters in her hand. "These are from him. We were great friends at school, but he married someone else, and I didn't see him for a long time after that. When the war started, everything changed. People were moving around a lot, and you never knew who you might bump into, especially in London."

Jack dragged a chair across the room and said, "Sit down, Mum. You're exhausted, and this sounds like the beginning of a long story."

Florence sat, dropping the letters into her lap. "You're right, it is a long story, and I'm too tired to go into it all now, so I'll just tell you a little. His name is Gordon and we ran into each other outside Hatchards on Piccadilly one rainy afternoon about a month before I met your father. We went somewhere for a cup of tea, and he told me that although his marriage wasn't a happy one, he was determined to stick it out. We were both desperately lonely. One thing led to another, and even though we only saw each other a few times, I got pregnant. I didn't tell him and didn't know how I was going to manage as a single mother, but then I met your father. He wanted to get married right away and leave London as soon as the war ended, so that's what we did."

"Do you think he ever suspected that Jack wasn't his?" Willow asked.

"If he did, he never said a word. You know Dad. Once he made a decision or a commitment, he never looked back. He did his duty and moved forward."

"Why did you keep writing letters to Gordon?" Jack asked. "What was the point?"

"When we parted for the last time, we agreed to stay in touch, just as friends. Neither of us ever wrote anything that his wife or your father couldn't have read without becoming alarmed. What I still haven't told you is that his wife passed away two years ago, and he's living alone in London now. His son, your half-brother, is grown, and Gordon wants me to move back to London to be with him. I've already decided to go. I'll have to sell the house because I need the money. Once I'm settled, you can both move over and we'll all be together. You've never been happy here, Jack, and Willow, you're really a Londoner now, after all the time you've spent there."

Willow stared at her in disbelief. They had been talking about Christmas decorations, and now her mother was talking about leaving Alaska forever. "Mum, I think you should slow down. Dad just died, and you don't know what you're doing."

"You're wrong. I've been thinking about this for years. I just never thought it would happen. This is really my last chance to be happy, and I intend to take it. I respected your father, even loved him in a certain way, and was grateful for all he did for us, but I've felt out of place since the day I got here. It's time for me to go home."

"I need to go outside and hang those lights. I can't take any more of this right now," Jack said. "I think my head is going to explode."

Willow stood up. "Mummy, I need to talk to Jeff." She followed Jack down the hall and went into the living room, where she picked up the phone and dialed the cannery.

An hour later, Jeff pulled up to their front door in his truck. Jack was on a ladder, stapling Christmas lights to the outside of the house. "You want some help with that?" he asked.

"No, thanks. I'm just putting up a few lights for Dad. He liked them."

Willow had been watching from the front window, her packed suitcases by her side. She raced out the door and threw herself into Jeff's arms as soon as she saw him. He lifted her off the ground and twirled her around, laughing, but then noticed the serious look on her face. "Hey, Babe, what's the matter?"

"Let's get going. It's such a long story. I'll tell you on the way. My suitcases are in there, by the door."

"Okay. Wait in the truck while I get them."

At eight that night, the winter solstice party at the Snowshoe was already in full swing. A lot of people had been there since the sun had set at three thirty and were planning to stay until it rose at ten fifteen the next morning. Bob and Eddie had promised blueberry pancakes, Bloody Marys, and reindeer sausages to anyone who managed to stay the whole time.

Keith and Tina were slow-dancing on one side of the dance floor. They hadn't been out for the evening since the kids had all come down with chickenpox back in October and were looking forward to making the most of it. They had offered Steve so much money to babysit all night that he couldn't refuse. Everyone knew there'd be no taxi, tow truck, or snowplow available that night. They'd have to fend for themselves if they were too drunk to drive home or skidded off the road.

Nancy and her girlfriend, Jane, were drinking beer at the bar and talking to Eddie about dogs. They had rescued Charlie from the trailer park and discovered he wasn't a vicious dog after all. Some training and a good home were all he needed to become a silly, lovable pet.

No one could believe their eyes when the door opened and Artie and his wife, Maureen, walked in. They stamped their feet, hung up their coats, and walked over to a table near the band as if they hadn't missed a night at the Snowshoe in years. Bob hurried over to greet them.

"Artie! Maureen! Great to see you. This really is a special occasion."

"It's the winter solstice, isn't it?" Maureen answered, smiling. "That's an occasion."

"Longest night of the year," Artie added. He winked at Maureen. "A good night for romance."

"Hush!" she said, kicking him under the table.

A bit later the door opened again and John, Sammy, Willow, and Jeff walked in. Sammy and John were carrying big, flat cardboard boxes which they set down gently on one end of the bar. They hung up their coats and sat down at a table next to Artie and Maureen. Jeff was wearing the jean jacket Willow had embroidered for him, the one people were always trying to buy because the design on the back was so unusual. Willow had piled her hair up on top of her head and was wearing a long rose-pink velvet dress with ivory lace trim that she had found in a vintage clothing shop in London.

Bob and Eddie were busy behind the bar, lining up bottles of champagne. Nancy and Jane began opening them carefully, not letting any of the precious wine spill on the floor. At a signal from Artie, the band stopped playing, and Jeff stood up.

"I've got some news," he said, looking around the room. "I just signed some papers today that will keep the cannery open until my new partner, Bill Scott, and I figure out what's going on with this cruise ship thing we've all heard about. Whatever happens after that, we're going to do what's best for Agate Cove and the people who live here. Bill lives in Seattle, and I know there was a rumor going around that I was planning to move down there, but I'm not. I'm staying right here."

They all clapped and cheered until Artie stood up and asked them to stop. Smiling, he said, "I think there's something else you all need to know." He nodded at the band and they began playing the Cat Stevens song "How Can I Tell You."

Willow and Jeff got up to dance. Her left hand had been in her dress pocket the whole time, but when they got to the center of the dance floor, she pulled it out and waved it in the air. On her ring finger was a gold band with three small gold forget-me-not flowers on it. Everyone crowded around to watch as Jeff took her in his arms.

Sammy walked over to the bar and opened the cardboard boxes while Nancy and Jane passed around glasses of champagne. "I've been making these since five this morning," he announced. "I hope you all appreciate that. As soon as this dance is over, I'm goin' home to bed." Inside the boxes were dozens of golden, fragile Norwegian krumkake, each one stamped with a delicate snowflake pattern.

Maureen jabbed Artie's arm. "You knew they were getting married today, didn't you?" she asked. "Why didn't you tell me?"

"I did, in a way. You just weren't paying attention. I said it was a good night for romance."

Out on the dance floor, Jeff whispered in Willow's ear, "Remember, it's the longest night of the year," and held her even closer.